WOMAN

Compiled by

SIDNEY S. SMITH

Salt Lake City, Utah

First Edition
January 1991

Second Edition
Revised and Enlarged
March 1991

ISBN 0-9622804-4-5

Library of Congress Catalog Card No. 90-091927

Sidney S. Smith
345 N. Davis Blvd.
Bountiful, Utah 84010

RESPECTFULLY
with sincere gratitude

Charlotte L. McCune Dean

and

E. Catherine Smith Scott

Contents

Also available by
Sidney S. Smith
In Love With Eloquence

SIDNEY S. SMITH

Mr. Smith was born in the rural community of Coalville, Utah, in 1928, and spent the first eleven years of his life there. Then his family moved to Pocatello, Idaho, and then to Ogden, Utah, where he made his home. He is a former paratrooper in the U. S. Army. He is married and has four daughters. As a marriage and family clinician and clinical therapist he takes great satisfaction in interacting with other people.

He admits that some of his most provocative experiences in life have come from within the covers of books. A gatherer of eloquence from around the world since his early years, he was led to publish a book in 1989 entitled "In Love With Eloquence." The format of "Eloquent Woman" is basically similar to the former, however, it is restricted to feminine eloquence, except for an interesting section on tributes to women by men, and also a section entitled "Language of Marriage" by both male and female.

INTRODUCTION

The literary legacy of the world has been greatly enriched by the contributions of women. Two styles of expression, male and female, each one unique and distinctive, provides us with an eloquent reservoir of invaluable writings. These priceless treasures are preserved with great care by generation after generation of thoughtful literary custodians. Women provide accurate insight into the more immediate emotional facets of life. Her concern and forte is emotional and logical. Both being basic characteristics of human existence.

Generally, she expressively and beautifully articulates faith, hope, love, and commitment. In her unpretentious manner she presents life's experiences and, her interpretation thereof, as a unique blend and consolidation of its processes and objectives. Common denominators in her writings are events and feeling responses. She speaks of people in general as one family, one race and civilization, and as ageless contemporaries throughout the pages of time.

Humanity, in general, is the loser for the literary discrimination of the female throughout time. Her bondage to family chores traditionally pre-empted her from serious writing efforts. The preponderance of today's literary treasury is of masculine origin. Avant garde female writers have begun to materialize slowly in recent centuries, and, as a writer, she is gradually taking her rightful place.

Motherhood provides many of the firsthand theses which females discourse about. Without her instinctual command of life which she so clearly grasps, along with a self-sacrificing benevolence to others, mankind would have ceased to exist. The female is a healing person, a consoling person, and a provider of comfort, and she, selflessly, provides nurturing sustenance to those about her.

Section five in *Eloquent Woman* contains tributes to women exclusively by men. Characteristically, men find women a ready-made subject to whom they readily and eloquently address themselves. Men use their finest words of praise and adulation as they speak endearingly of their sweethearts, mothers, and closest of companions. The reader should find this material to be one of the finest collections of tributes to women to be found anywhere. It is an eloquent tribute to that gender of the human race who has been described as "the one who makes life worth living."

The sixth section, Language of Marriage, is dedicated to commentaries by both male and female on and about the institution of marriage. It is not advisory as such, but appreciatory and commendatory in nature. This, also, is possibly one of the few collections of this nature to be found anywhere.

Some of my own thoughts have been interspersed throughout this volume. I lay no claim to fame for them, and hope, you the reader, will tolerate their presence as much as others from the recognized great and prominent writers presented herein.

—Sidney S. Smith

ACKNOWLEDGEMENTS

My hat goes off to the eloquent language of the female of the human species. Her expressions, in whatever form you may find them, are exactly what and how one would expect them to be. They uphold the fact that they are wizards with words, and have incisive, sharp minds. Her written legacy well proves her ability to accommodate in writing her great breadth of imagination and thought for which she is well known.

In *Eloquent Woman* I have attempted to bring out the best of the extant treasury of feminine poetry, songs, famous comments, and ideas throughout time. I am grateful that so many women have preserved the evidence of these skills by leaving them with us in poetry and prose form.

As in my recent book *In Love With Eloquence*, I have drawn from many sources to bring together this singular treasury of writings which, on their own merit, have become dear to the hearts of people all over the world. This unique collection is one of a kind. It will not be found in any other volume anywhere.

This volume contains the literary best of the best. I extend my warmest appreciation to women whose works, small and great, are included herein. Without her tireless efforts to, in the first place, be persuasive, and, in the second place, to chronicle her thoughts, this volume would not exist.

"Euclid Alone," "First Fig," "Travel," "God's World," "Prayer to Persephone," "Not in a Silver Casket," "Recuerdo," and an excerpt from "Renascence" by Edna St. Vincent Millay. Copyright © 1917, 1921, 1922, 1931, 1945, 1948, 1950, 1958 by Edna St. Vincent Millay and Norma Millay Ellis. Reprinted by permission of Elizabeth Barnett, Literary Executor. I am indebted to The Church of Jesus Christ of Latter-day Saints for their permission to use the words to "I Am a Child of God," by Naomi Randall.

Many thanks to Paula Conway, typesetter, for her patience and great skills, and to Bill Kuhre, artist, for cover design. Also, others who volunteered items to be included, and who have provided hours of research in correcting and locating certain parts of the contents. Many have provided moral support to me in proceeding with this project. Their support has been an invaluable help and service to me. Thank you.

Elizabeth Barrett Browning (1806-1861)

Alice Cary (1820-1871)

Queen Elizabeth (1533-1603)

Mary Howitt (1799-1888)

Winifred Letts (1882-c. 1936)

Edna Wheeler Wilcox (1855-1919)

**Jane Austen
(1775-1817)**

**Charlotte Bronte
(1816-1855)**

Anna Hempstead Branch
(1879-1937)

Elizabeth Coatsworth
(1893-   )

Emily (Elizabeth) Dickinson
(1830-1886)

Rachel Field
(1894-1942)

Queen Isabella
(1451-1504)

Helen (Adams) Keller
(1880-1968)

Emma Lazarus
(1849-1887)

Amy Lowell
(1874-1925)

Edna St. Vincent Millay
(1892-1950)

Sarah Teasdale
(1884-1933)

Rachel Louise Carson (1907-1964)

Eleanor Roosevelt (1884-1962)

1

LOVE OF COUNTRY AND PATRIOTISM

We would rather starve than sell our national honor.

Indira Netira Gandhi (1917-1984)

AMERICA THE BEAUTIFUL

Oh, beautiful for spacious skies,
For amber waves of grain,
For purple mountain majesties
Above the fruited plain!

America! America!
God shed his grace on thee,
And crown thy good with brotherhood
From sea to shining sea.

Oh, beautiful for pilgrim feet,
Whose stern impassioned stress
A thoroughfare of freedom beat
Across the wilderness!

America! America!
God mend thine every flaw,
Confirm thy soul in self control,
Thy liberty in law.

Oh, beautiful for heroes proved
In liberating strife,
Who more than self their country loved,
And mercy more than life!

America! America!
May God thy gold refine,
Till all success be nobleness,
And every gain divine.

Oh, beautiful for patriot dream
That sees beyond the years
Thine alabaster cities gleam,
Undimmed by human tears!

America! America!
God shed his grace on thee,
And crown thy good with brotherhood
From sea to shining sea.

Katherine Lee Bates (1859-1929)

MY GLORY

Though God hath raised me high, yet this I count the glory of my crown: that I have reigned with your loves.

Elizabeth I, Queen of England (1533-1603)

NEW COLOSSUS

Not like the brazen giant of Greek fame
With conquering limbs astride from land to land;
Here, at our sea-washed, sunset gates shall stand
A mighty woman with a torch, whose flame
Is the imprisoned lightning, and her name
Mother of exiles.
From her beacon-hand
Glows world-wide welcome;
Her mild eyes command
The air-bridged harbor that twin cities frame.
"Keep, ancient lands, your storied pomp!" cries she
With silent lips. "Give me your tired, your poor,
Your huddled masses yearning to breathe free,
The wretched refuse of your teeming shore.
Send these, the homeless, tempest tossed to me.
I lift my lamp beside the Golden Door!"

Emma Lazarus (1849-1887)

THE SPIRES OF OXFORD

I saw the spires of Oxford
    As I was passing by,
The grey spires of Oxford
    Against a pearl-gray sky;
My heart was with the Oxford men
    Who went abroad to die.

The years go fast at Oxford,
    The golden years and gay;
The hoary colleges look down
    On careless boys at play,
But when the bugles sounded — War!
    They put their games away.

They left the peaceful river,
    The cricket field, the quad,
The shaven lawns of Oxford,
    To seek a bloody sod.
They gave their merry youth away
    For country and for God.

God rest you, happy gentlemen,
    Who laid your good lives down,
Who took the khaki and the gun
    Instead of cap and gown.
God bring you to a fairer place
    Than even Oxford town.

Winifred Letts (1882]c. 1936)

LIBERTY

O Liberty! O Liberty!
What crimes are committed in thy name.

Madame Roland (1754-1793)

SEA AND AIR

The use of the sea and air is common to all; neither can a title to the ocean belong to any people or private persons, forasmuch as neither nature nor public use and custom permit any possession thereof.

Elizabeth I, Queen of England (1533-1603)

FIRST THANKSGIVING

Peace and Mercy and Jonathan,
And Patience (very small),
Stood by the table giving thanks
The first Thanksgiving of all.
There was very little for them to eat,
Nothing special and nothing sweet;
Only bread and a little broth,
And a bit of fruit (and no tablecloth);
But Peace and Mercy and Jonathan
And Patience in a row,
Stood up and asked a blessing on
Thanksgiving, long ago.
Thankful they were their ship had come
Safely across the sea;
Thankful they were for hearth and home,
And kin and company;
They were glad of broth to go with their bread,
Glad their apples were round and red,
Glad of mayflowers they would bring
Out of the woods again next spring.
So Peace and Mercy and Jonathan,
And Patience (very small),
Stood up gratefully giving thanks
The first Thanksgiving of all.

Nancy Byrd Turner (1880-   )

LANDING OF THE PILGRIMS

The breaking waves dashed high
    On a stern and rock-bound coast,
And the woods against a stormy sky
    Their giant branches tossed;

And the heavy night hung dark
    The hills and waters o'er,
When a band of exiles moored their bark
    On a wild New England shore.

Not as the conqueror comes,
    They, the true-hearted, came;
Not with the roll of stirring drums,
    And the trumpet that sings of fame;

Not as the flying come,
    In silence and in fear;—
They shook the depths of the desert's gloom
    With their hymns of lofty cheer.

Amidst the storm they came,
    And the stars heard, and the sea;
And the sounding aisles of the dim woods rang
    To the anthem of the free!

The ocean-eagle soared
    From his nest by the white wave's foam,
And the rocking pines of the forest roared;
    This was their welcome home!

There were men with hoary hair
    Amidst that pilgrim band;
Why had they come to wither there,
    Away from their childhood's land?

There was woman's fearless eye,
    Lit by her deep love's truth;
There was manhood's brow, serenely high,
    And the fiery heart of youth.

What sought they thus afar?
    Bright jewels of the mine?
The wealth of seas, the spoils of war?—
    They sought a faith's pure shrine!

Aye! call it holy ground,
    The soil where first they trod!
They left unstained what there they found—
    Freedom to worship God!

Felicia Dorothea Hemans (1793-1835)

TAMED

The axe has cut the forest down,
The laboring ox has smoothed all clear,
Apples now grow where pine trees stood,
And slow cows graze instead of deer.

Where Indian fires once raised their smoke
The chimneys of a farmhouse stand,
And cocks crow barnyard challenges
To dawns that once saw savage land.

The axe, the plow, the binding wall,
By these the wilderness is tamed,
By these the white man's will is wrought,
The rivers bridged, the new towns named.

Elizabeth Coatsworth (1893-   )

DESIRE

I am no lover of pompous title, but only desire that my name may be recorded in a line or two, which shall briefly express my name, my virginity, the years of my reign, the reformation of religion under it, and my preservation of peace.

Elizabeth I, Queen of England (1533-1603)

LINCOLN

There was a boy of other days,
A quiet, awkward, earnest lad,
Who trudged long weary miles to get
A book on which his heart was set—
And then no candle had!

He was too poor to buy a lamp
But very wise in woodmen's ways.
He gathered seasoned bough and stem,
And crisping leaf, and kindled them
Into a ruddy blaze.

Then as he lay full length and read,
The firelight flickered on his face,
And etched his shadow on the gloom,
And made a picture in the room,
In that most humble place.

The hard years came, the hard years went,
But, gentle, brave, and strong of will,
He met them all. And when today
We see his pictured face, we say,
"There's light upon it still."

Nancy Byrd Turner (1880-   )

SPANISH JOHNNY

The old West, the old time,
    The old wind singing through
The red, red grass a thousand miles—
    And, Spanish Johnny, you!
He'd sit beside the water ditch
    When all his herd was in,
And never mind a child, but sing
    To his mandolin.

The big stars, the blue night,
    The moon-enchanted lane;
The olive man who never spoke,
    But sang the songs of Spain.
His speech with men was wicked talk—
    To hear it was a sin;
But those were golden things he said
    To his mandolin.

The gold songs, the gold stars,
    The word so golden then;
And the hand so tender to a child—
    Had killed so many men.

He died a hard death long ago
    Before the road came in—
The night before he swung, he sang
    To his mandolin.

Willa Sibert Cather (1876-1947)

BATTLE HYMN OF THE REPUBLIC

Mine eyes have seen the glory of the coming of the Lord;
He is trampling out the vintage where the grapes of wrath are
    stored.
He hath loosed the fateful lightning of His terrible swift
    sword;
        His truth is marching on.

I have seen Him in the watch-fires of a hundred circling
    camps;
They have builded him an altar in the evening dews and
    damps;
I can read His righteous sentence by the dim and flaring
    lamps;
        His day is marching on.

I have read a fiery gospel, writ in burnished rows of steel:
"As ye deal with my contemners, so with you my grace shall
    deal;
Let the Hero, born of woman, crush the serpent with his
    heel,
        Since God is marching on."

He has sounded forth the trumpet that shall never call
    retreat;
He is sifting out the hearts of men before his judgment-seat:
Oh, be swift, my soul, to answer Him! be jubilant my feet!
        Our God is marching on.

In the beauty of the lilies Christ was born across the sea,
With a glory in His bosom that transfigures you and me;
As He died to make men holy, let us die to make men free,
        While God is marching on.

Julia Ward Howe (1819-1910)

WASHINGTON

He played by the river when he was young,
He raced with rabbits along the hills,
He fished for minnows, and climbed and swung,
And hooted back at the whippoorwills.
Strong and slender and tall he grew —
And then, one morning, the bugles blew.

Over the hills the summons came,
Over the river's shining rim.
He said that the bugles called his name,
He knew that his country needed him,
And he answered, "Coming!" and marched away
For many a night and many a day.

Perhaps when the marches were hot and long
He'd think of the river flowing by
Or, camping under the winter sky,
Would hear the whippoorwill's far-off song.
Boy or soldier, in peace or strife,
He loved America all his life!

Nancy Byrd Turner (1880-   )

INNER STRENGTH

I know I have the body of a weak and feeble woman, but I have the heart and stomach of a king, and of a king of England too; and think foul scorn that Parma or Spain, or any prince of Europe should dare to invade the borders of my realm.

Elizabeth I, Queen of England (1533-1603)
to her troops at the approach of the Spanish Armada, 1588.

BRAVE OLD WORLD

When the last H-bomb blast has done its stuff
And stilled for good the Geiger counter's voice,
When nothing's left but just a few of us
Will come the moment of my dreadful choice:
Invent the peaceful wheel? Oh dear me, no!
Let those who would, assuage the general woe—
I plan to freeze my neighbors to the marrow
By being the inventor of the bow and arrow.

                                    Elisabeth Lambert

ALL QUIET ALONG THE POTOMAC

"All quiet along the Potomac," they say,
    "Except, now and then, a stray picket
Is shot, as he walks on his beat to and fro,
    By a rifleman hid in the thicket."
'Tis nothing—a private or two now and then
    Will not count in the news of the battle;
Not an officer lost—only one of the men,
    Moaning out, all alone, the death-rattle.

All quiet along the Potomac to-night,
    Where the soldiers lie peacefully dreaming;
Their tents, in the rays of the clear autumn moon
    Or the light of the watch-fire, are gleaming.
A tremulous sigh of the gentle night-wind
    Through the forest-leaves softly is creeping,
While stars up above, with their glittering eyes,
    Keep guard, for the army is sleeping.

There's only the sound of the lone sentry's tread
    As he tramps from the rock to the fountain,

And thinks of the two in the low trundle-bed
    Far away in the cot on the mountain.
His musket falls slack; his face, dark and grim,
    Grows gentle with memories tender
As he mutters a prayer for the children asleep—
    For their mother; may Heaven defend her!

The moon seems to shine just as brightly as then,
    That night when the love yet spoken
Leaped up to his lips—when low-murmured vows
    Were pledged to be ever unbroken.
Then, drawing his sleeve roughly over his eyes,
    He dashes off tears that are welling,
And gathers his gun closer up to its place,
    As if to keep down the heart-swelling.

He passes the fountain, the blasted pine tree,
    The footstep is lagging and weary;
Yet onward he goes through the broad belt of light,
    Toward the shade of the forest so dreary.
Hark! was it the night-wind that rustled the leaves?
    Was it moonlight so wondrously flashing?
It looked like a rifle—"Ha! Mary, good-bye!"
    The red life-blood is ebbing and plashing.

All quiet along the Potomac to-night,
    No sound save the rush of the river;
While soft falls the dew on the face of the dead—
    The picket's off duty for ever!

Ethel Lynn Beers (1827-1879)

BASIC PRINCIPLES

The right to criticize.
The right to hold unpopular beliefs.
The right to protest.
The right of independent thought.

Margaret Chase Smith (1898-   )

A SONG FOR OUR FLAG

A bit of color against the blue:
Hues of the morning, blue for true,
And red for the kindling light of flame,
And white for a nation's stainless fame.
Oh! fling it forth to the winds afar,
With hope in its every shining star:
Under its folds wherever found,
Thank God, we have freedom's holy ground.

Don't you love it, as out it floats
From the schoolhouse peak, and glad young throats
Sing of the banner that aye shall be
Symbol of honor and victory?
Don't you thrill when the marching feet
Of jubilant soldiers shake the street,
And the bugles shrill, and the trumpets call,
And the red, white and blue is over us all?
Don't you pray, amid starting tears,
It may never be furled through age-long years?

A song for our flag, our country's boast,
That gathers beneath it a mighty host;
Long may it wave o'er the goodly land
We hold in fee 'neath our Father's hand.
For God and liberty evermore
May that banner stand from shore to shore,
Never to those high meanings lost,
Never with alien standards crossed,
But always valiant and pure and true,
Our starry flag: red, white, and blue.

Margaret E. Sangster (1838-1912)

Join the union, girls, and together say *"Equal Pay for Equal Work."*

Susan B. Anthony (1820-1906)

SONG OF THE SETTLERS

Freedom is a hard-bought thing—
A gift no man can give,
For some, a way of dying,
For most, a way to live.

Freedom is a hard-bought thing—
A rifle in the hand,
The horses hitched at sunup,
A harvest in the land.

Freedom is a hard-bought thing—
A massacre, a bloody route,
The candles lit at nightfall,
And the night shut out.

Freedom is a hard-bought thing—
An arrow in the back,
The wind in the long corn rows,
And the hay in the rack.

Freedom is a way of living,
A song, a mighty cry.
Freedom is the bread we eat;
Let it be the way we die.

Jessamyn West

HOLLY

But give me holly, bold and jolly,
Honest, prickly, shining holly;
Pluck me holly leaf and berry
For the day when I make merry.

Christina Georgina Rossetti (1830-1894), from *Sing Song*

ROMAN GIRL'S SONG
(Excerpts)

Rome, Rome! thou art no more
    As thou hast been!
On thy seven hills yore
    Thou sat'st a queen.

Thou hadst thy triumphs then
    Purpling the street,
Leaders and sceptred men
    Bowed at thy feet.

They that thy mantle wore,
    As gods were seen,—
Rome, Rome! thou art no more
    As thou hast been!

Rome! thine imperial brow
    Never shall rise:
What hast thou left thee now!—
    Thou hast thy skies!

Blue, deeply blue, they are,
    Gloriously bright!
Veiling thy wastes afar
    With colored light.

Thou hast fair forms that move
    With queenly tread;
Thou hast proud fanes above
    Thy mighty dead.

Yet wears thy Tiber's shore
    A mournful mien:—
Rome, Rome! thou art no more
    As thou hast been!

Felicia Hemans (1793-1835)

2

FAMILY, HOME AND NATURE

If I can stop one heart from breaking,
I shall not live in vain;
If I can ease one life the aching,
Or cool one pain,
Or help one fainting robin
Unto his nest again,
I shall not live in vain.

Emily Dickinson (1830-1886)

MY KATE

She was not as pretty as women I know,
And yet all your best made of sunshine and snow
Drop to shade, melt to nought in the long-trodden ways,
While she's still remembered on warm and cold days—
                              My Kate.

Her air had a meaning, her movements a grace;
You turned from the fairest to gaze on her face;
And when you had once seen her forehead and mouth,
You saw as distinctly her soul and her truth—
                              My Kate.

Such a blue inner light from her eyelids outbroke,
You looked at her silence and fancied she spoke;
When she did, so peculiar yet soft was the tone,
Though the loudest spoke also, you heard her alone—
                              My Kate.

I doubt that she said to you much that could act
As a thought of suggestion; she did not attract
In the sense of the brilliant or wise; I infer
'Twas her thinking of others made you think of her—
                              My Kate.

She never found fault with you, never implied
Your wrong by her right; and yet men at her side
Grew nobler, girls purer, as though the whole town
The children were gladder that pulled at her gown—
                              My Kate.

None knelt at her feet confessed lovers in thrall;
They knelt more to God than they used—that was all;
If you praised her as charming, some asked what you meant,
But the charm of her presence was felt when she went—
                              My Kate.

The weak and the gentle, the ribald and rude,
She took as she found them, and did them all good;
It always was so with her—see what you have!
She has made the grass greener even here with her grave—
My Kate.

Elizabeth Barrett Browning (1806-1861)

WOMAN

A woman is a foreign land,
Of which, though there he settle young,
A man will ne'er quite understand
The customs, politics, and tongue.

Coventry Patmore (1823-1896), from "Woman"

ANNE

Her eyes be like the violets,
    Ablow in Sudbury Lane;
When she doth smile her face is sweet
    As blossoms after rain;
With grief I think of my gray hairs,
    And wish me young again.

In comes she through the dark old door
    Upon this Sabbath day;
And she doth bring the tender wind
    That sings in bush and tree;
And hints of all the apple boughs
    That kissed her by the way.

Our person stands up straight and tall,
    For our dear souls to pray,

And of the place where sinners go,
    Some gruesome things to say;
Now she is highest Heaven to me;
    So Hell is far away.

Most stiff and still the good folk sit
    To hear the sermon through;
But if our God be such a God,
    And if these things be true,
Why did he make her then so fair,
    And both her eyes so blue?

A flickering light, the sun creeps in,
    And finds her sitting there;
And touches soft her lilac gown,
    And soft her yellow hair;
I look across to that old pew,
    And have both praise and prayer.

O violets in Sudbury Lane,
    Amid the grasses green,
This maid who stirs ye with her feet
    Is far more fair I ween!
I wonder how my forty years
    Look by her sweet sixteen.

                      Lizette Woodworth Reese (1856-1935)

MOTHER

Who ran to help me when I fell,
And would some pretty story tell,
Or kiss the place to make it well?
    My mother.

                      Jane Taylor (1783-1824)

A LADY

You are beautiful and faded
Like an old opera tune
Played upon a harpsichord;
Or like the sun-flooded silks
Of an eighteenth century boudoir.
In your eyes
Smoulder the fallen roses of out-lived minutes,
And the perfume of your soul
Is vague and suffusing,
With the pungence of sealed spice-jars.
Your half-tones delight me,
And I grow mad with gazing
At your blent colours.

My vigour is a new-minted penny,
Which I cast at your feet.
Gather it up from the dust,
That its sparkle may amuse you.

Amy Lowell (1874-1925)

BRIGHT STAR

A young star which shone o'er life too bright an image for such glass! A lovely being scarcely formed or moulded; a rose with all its leaves yet folded.

Harriet Beecher Stowe (1811-1896), from Uncle Tom's Cabin

ONE MOTHER

Most of all the other beautiful things in life come by twos and threes, by dozens, and hundreds. Plenty of roses, stars, sunsets, rainbows, brothers and sisters, aunts and cousins, but only one mother in the whole world.

Kate Douglas Wiggin (1856-1923)

MY LOVE

How do I love thee? Let me count the ways.
I love thee to the depth, and breadth, and height
My soul can reach, when feeling out of sight
For the ends of being and ideal Grace.
I love thee to the level of every day's
Most quiet need, by sun and candle-light.
I love thee freely, as men strive for Right;
I love thee purely, as they turn from Praise.
I love thee with the passion put to use
In my old griefs, and with my childhood's faith.
I love thee with a love I seem to lose
With my lost saints, I love thee with the breath,
Smiles, tears, of all my life!—and, if God choose,
I shall love thee better after death.

> Elizabeth Barrett Browning (1806-1861),
> from "Sonnets from the Portuguese"

NOT IN A SILVER CASKET

Not in a silver casket cool with pearls
Or rich with red corundum or with blue,
Locked, and the key withheld, as other girls
Have given their loves, I give my love to you;
Not in a lover's-knot, not in a ring
Worked in such fashion, and the legend plain—
Semper Fidelis, where a secret spring
Kennels a drop of mischief for the brain;
Love in the open hand, no thing but that,
Ungemmed, unhidden, wishing not to hurt,
As one should bring you cowslips in a hat
Swung from the hand, or apples in her skirt,
I bring you, calling out as children do:
"Look what I have!"—And these are all for you.

> Edna St. Vincent Millay (1892-1950)

THE VICTORY OF SAMOTHRACE SPEAKS TO THE MUTILATED OF THE GREAT WAR

What could flesh do, in fight so unfair?
I lay . . . I too . . . in a tomb of despair.
White over ruin I shine in the air.

I knew the damnation of body and will . . .
Decapitation . . . swords could not kill!
Wings for salvation, remain with me still.

Now I have done with laurel and blade;
All that I won with my losses is laid:
I soar to the sun, with my soul unafraid.

Oblivion lies upon navies and kings,
And armies with eyes upon temporal things . . .
I shine in the skies, upon triumphant wings.

Ellen Glines, inspired by the Greek statue
"Winged Victory of Samothrace" in the Louvre, Paris

WORTH

An emerald is as green as grass;
    A ruby red as blood;
A sapphire shines as blue as heaven;
    A flint lies in the mud.

A diamond is a brilliant stone,
    To catch the world's desire;
An opal holds a fiery spark;
    But a flint holds fire.

Christina Georgina Rossetti, *Sing-Song* (1830-1894)

LET NO CHARITABLE HOPE

Now let no charitable hope
Confuse my mind with images
Of eagle and antelope:
I am in nature none of these.

I was, being human, born alone;
I am, being woman, hard beset;
I live by squeezing from a stone
The little nourishment I get.

In masks outrageous and austere
The years go by in single file;
But none has merited my fear,
And none has escaped my smile.

Elinore Wylie (1885-1928)

TRAVEL

The railroad track is miles away,
And the day is loud with voices speaking,
Yet there isn't a train goes by all day
But I hear its whistle shrieking.

All night there isn't a train goes by,
Though the night is still for sleep and dreaming,
But I see its cinders red on the sky,
And hear its engine steaming.

My heart is warm with the friends I make,
And better friends I'll not be knowing;
Yet there isn't a train I wouldn't take,
No matter where it's going.

Edna St. Vincent Millay (1892-1950)

PURITAN LADY

Wild Carthage held her, Rome,
  Sidon. She stared to tears
Tall, golden Helen, wearying
  Behind the Trojan spears.

Towered Antwerp knew her well;
  She wore her quiet gown
In her hushed house in Oxford grass,
  Or lane in Salem town.

Humble and high in one,
  Cool, ceratin, different,
She lasts; scarce saint, yet half a child,
  As hard as innocent.

What grave, long afternoons,
  What caged airs around her blown,
Stripped her of humor, left her bare
  As cloud, or wayside stone?

Made her as clear a thing,
  In this slack world as plain
As a white flower on a grave,
  Or sleet sharp at a pane?

Lizette Woodworth Reese (1856-1935)

HIDDEN WEALTH

The Golden-rod is one of the fairy magic flowers; it grows not up to seek human love amid the day, but to mark to the discerning what wealth lies hid in the secret caves of the earth.

Margaret Fuller (Ossoli) (1810-1850), from her journal, September 1840

COMMON INFERENCE

A night: mysterious, tender, quiet, deep;
Heavy with flowers; full of life asleep;
Thrilling with insect voices; thick with stars;
No cloud between the dewdrops and red Mars;
The small earth whirling softly on her way,
The moonbeams and the waterfalls at play;
A million million worlds that move in peace,
A million mighty laws that never cease;
And one small ant-heap, hidden by small weeds,
Rich with eggs, slaves, and store of millet seeds.
   They sleep beneath the sod
     And trust in God.

A day: all glorious, royal, blazing bright;
Heavy with flowers; full of life and light;
Great fields of corn and sunshine; courteous trees;
Snow-sainted mountains; earth-embracing seas;
Wide golden deserts; slender silver streams;
Clear rainbows where the tossing fountain gleams;
And everywhere, in happiness and peace,
A million forms of life that never cease;
And one small ant-heap, crushed by passing tread,
Hath scarce enough alive to mourn the dead!
   They shriek beneath the sod,
     "There is no God!"

Charlotte Perkins Stetson Gilman (1860-1935)

HELPLESS

Never does one feel oneself so utterly helpless as in trying
to speak comfort for great bereavement. I will not try it. Time
is the only comforter for the loss of a mother.

Jane Welsh Carlyle (1801-1866), from a letter to Thomas Carlyle

HOMAGE

Before me you bowed as before an altar,
And I reached down and drew you to my bosom;
Proud of your reverence, and reverence returning,
But craving most your love and not your awe.

My hands about your head curved themselves as
    holding
A treasure, fragile and of glad possession;
Dear were the bones of your skull beneath my fingers,
And I grew brave at thought of your defense.

Not as a man I felt you in my brooding,
But as a babe of my own body;
Precious your worth, but dearer your dependence;
Almost I wished to feed you at my breast.

And not to me, I knew, belonged your homage:
I but the vessel of your holy drinking;
The channel to you of that ancient wonder
Of love and womanhood, I but a woman.

Then never need your memory be shamefaced
That I have seen your flesh at worship;
Do you think I did not kneel when you were kneeling?
Even lowlier bowed my head, and bowed my heart.

                                  Helen Hoyt (1887-   )

SPRINGTIME

Buttercups and daisies.
    Oh, the pretty flowers;
Coming ere the Springtime,
    To tell of sunny hours.

Mary Howitt (1799-1888), from "Buttercups and Daisies"

GRIEVE NOT, LADIES

Oh, grieve not, Ladies, if at night
    Ye wake to feel your beauty going.
It was a web of frail delight.
    Inconstant as an April snowing.

In other eyes, in other lands,
    In deep fair pools, new beauty lingers,
But like spent water in your hands
    It runs from your reluctant fingers.

Ye shall not keep the singing lark
    That owes to earlier skies its duty.
Weep not to hear along the dark
    The sound of your departing beauty.

The fine and anguished ear of night
    Is tuned to hear the smallest sorrow.
Oh, wait until the morning light!
    It may not seem so gone tomorrow!

But honey-pale and rosy-red!
    Brief lights that made a little shining!
Beautiful looks about us shed—
    They leave us to the old repining.

Think not the watchful dim despair
    Has come to you, the first, sweet-hearted!
For oh, the gold in Helen's hair!
    And how she cried when that was parted.

Perhaps that one that took the most,
    The swiftest borrower, wildest spender,
May count, as we do not, the cost—
    And grow to us more true and tender.

Happy are we if in his eyes
    We see no shadow of forgetting,
Nay—if our star sinks in those skies
    We shall not wholly see its setting.

Then let us laugh as do the brooks
    That such immortal youth is ours,
If memory keeps for them our looks
    As fresh as are the spring-time flowers.

Oh, grieve not, ladies, if at night
    Ye wake to feel the cold December!
Rather recall the early light
    And in your loved one's arms, remember.

Anna Hempstead Branch (1874-1937)

DOWN THE BAYOU

The cypress swamp around me wraps its spell
With hushing sounds in moss-hung branches there,
Like congregations rushing down to prayer,
While Solitude, like some unsounded bell,
Hangs full of secrets that it cannot tell,
And leafy litanies on the humid air
Intone themselves, and on the tree-trunks bare
The scarlet lichen writes her rubrics well.
The cypress-knees take on them marvelous shapes
Of pygmy nuns, gnomes, goblins, witches, fays,
The vigorous vine the withered gum-tree drapes,
Across the oozy ground the rabbit plays,
The moccasin to jungle depths escapes,
And through the gloom the wild deer shyly gaze.

Mary Ashley Townsend (1832-1901)

WHAT IS HOME WITHOUT A MOTHER?

What is home without a mother?
What are all the joys we meet,
When her loving smile no longer
Greets the coming, coming of our feet?
The days seem long, the nights are drear,
And time rolls slowly on:
And oh! how few are childhood's pleasures,
When her gentle, gentle care is gone.

Things we prize are first to vanish,
Hearts we love to pass away;
And how soon e'en in our childhood,
We behold her turning, turning grey:
Her eye grows dim, her step is slow;
Her joys of earth are past;
And sometimes e'er we learn to know her,
She hath breathed on earth her last.

Older hearts may have their sorrows,
Griefs that quickly die away,
But a mother lost in childhood
Grieves the heart, the heart from day to day;
We miss her kind, her willing hand,
Her fond and earnest care;
And oh! how dark is life around us,
What is home without her there.

Alice Hawthorne

Of the southwind, sweet and low;
Never yet was a springtime
When the buds forgot to blow.

Margaret E. Sangster (1839-1912)

CONSERVATIVE

The garden beds I wandered by
    One bright and cheerful morn,
When I found a new-fledged butterfly,
    A-sitting on a thorn,
A black and crimson butterfly
    All doleful and forlorn.

I thought that life could have no sting
    To infant butterflies,
So I gazed on this unhappy thing
    With wonder and surprise,
While sadly with his waving wing
    He wiped his weeping eyes.

Said I, "What can the matter be?
    Why weepest thou so sore?
With garden fair and sunlight free
    And flowers in goodly store,"—
But he only turned away from me
    And burst into a roar.

Cried he, "My legs are thin and few
    Where once I had a swarm!
Soft fuzzy fur—a joy to view—
    Once kept my body warm,
Before these flapping wing-things grew,
    To hamper and deform!"

At that outrageous bug I shot
    The fury of mine eye;
Said I, in scorn all burning hot,
    In rage and anger high,
"You ignominious idiot!
    Those wings are made to fly!"

"I do not want to fly," said he,
    "I only want to squirm!"
And he drooped his wings dejectedly,
    But still his voice was firm:
"I do not want to be a fly!
    I want to be a worm!"

O yesterday of unknown lack,
    Today of unknown bliss!
I left my fool in red and black;
    The last I saw was this,—
The creature madly climbing back
    Into his chrysalis.

Charlotte Perkins Stetson Gilman (1860-1935)

TEARS

(a sonnet)

When I consider Life and its few years—
A wisp of fog betwixt us and the sun;
A call to battle, and the battle done
Ere the last echo dies within our ears;
A rose choked in the grass; an hour of fears;
The gusts that past a darkening shore do beat;
The burst of music down an unlistening street,—
I wonder at the idleness of tears.
Ye old, old dead, and ye of yesternight,
Chieftains, and bards, and keepers of the sheep,
By every cup of sorrow that you had,
Loose me from tears, and make me see aright
How each has back what once he stayed to weep:
Homer his sight, David his little lad!

Lizette Woodworth Reese (1856-1935)

EACH DAY

I'll tell you how the sun rose,—
A ribbon at a time.
The steeples swam in amethyst,
The news like squirrels ran.

The hills untied their bonnets,
The bobolinks begun.
Then I said softly to myself,
"That must have been the sun!"

But how he set, I know not.
There seemed a purple stile
Which little yellow boys and girls
Were climbing all the while

Till when they reached the other side,
A dominie in gray
Put gently up the evening bars
And led the flock away.

Emily Dickinson (1830-1886)

AWAY

The little rose is dust, my dear;
The elfin wind is gone
That sang a song of silver words
And cooled our hearts with dawn.

And what is left to hope, my dear,
Or what is left to say?
The rose, the little wind and you
Have gone so far away.

Grace Hazard Conkling (1878-1958)

RAILWAY

I like to see it lap the miles,
And lick the valleys up,
And stop to feed itself at tanks;
And then, prodigious, step

Around a pile of mountains,
And, supercilious, peer
In shanties by the side of roads;
And then a quarry pare

To fit its sides, and crawl between,
Complaining all the while
In horrid, hooting stanza;
Then chase itself down hill

And neigh like Boanerges;
Then, punctual as a star,
Stop—docile and omnipotent—
At its own stable door.

Emily Dickinson (1830-1886)

FUTILITY

I made you many and many a song,
Yet never one told all you are—
It was as though a net of words
Were flung to catch a star;

It was as though I curved my hand
And dipped sea-water eagerly,
Only to find it lost the blue
Dark splendor of the sea.

Sarah Teasdale (1884-1933)

OLD SAUL

I cannot think of any word
To make it plain to you,
How white a thing the hawthorne bush
That delicately blew

Within a crook of Tinges Lane;
Each May Day there it stood;
And lit a flame of loveliness
For the small neighborhood.

So fragile-white a thing it was,
I cannot make it plain;
Or the sweet fumbling of the bees,
Like the break in a rain.

Old Saul lived near. And this his life—
To cobble for his bread;
To mourn a tall son lost at sea,
A daughter worse than dead.

And so, in place of all his lack,
He set the hawthorne tree;
Made it his wealth, his mirth, his god,
His Zion to touch and see.

Born English he. Down Tinges Lane
His lad's years came and went;
He saw, out there behind his thorn,
A hundred thorns of Kent.

At lovers slipping through the dusk
He shook a lover's head;
Grudged them each flower. It was too white
For any but the dead.

Once on a blurred, wet, silver day
He said to two or three:
"Folks, when I go, pluck yonder bloom
That I may take with me."

But it was winter when he went,
The road wind-drenched and torn;
They laid upon his coffin lid
A wreath made all of thorn.

Lizette Woodworth Reese (1856-1935)

MINIATURE

Because the little gentleman made nautical instruments
And lived in a street which ran down to the sea,
The neighbors called him "Salt Charlie."
I wonder what they would have said if they had known
That he stole out every evening to a sweet shop
And bought sticks of red-and-white sugar candy.
It was a pleasant thing to see him,
Standing meekly before the custom-house,
Sucking a sugar-stick,
And gazing at the dead funnels of anchored steamers
Against a star-sprung sky.

I thought of him in an oval gilt frame
Against sprigged wall-paper,
Done in Fra Angelico pinks and blues
Of a clear and sprightly elegance.
Wherefore, being convinced of his value as ornament,
I have set him on paper for the delectation
Of sundry scattered persons
Who consider such things important.

Amy Lowell (1874-1925)

GOD'S WORLD

O world, I cannot hold thee close enough!
Thy winds, thy wide grey skies!
Thy mists, that roll and rise!
Thy woods, this autumn day, that ache and sag
And all but cry with colour! That gaunt crag
To crush! To lift the lean of that black bluff!
World, World, I cannot get thee close enough!

Long have I known a glory in it all,
But never knew I this:
Here such a passion is
As stretcheth me apart,—Lord, I do fear
Thou'st made the world too beautiful this year;
My soul is all but out of me,—let fall
No burning leaf; prithee, let no bird call.

Edna St. Vincent Millay (1892-1950)

TOMBSTONE

Under this sod and beneath these trees
Lies the body of Solomon Pease.
He's not here, just his pod;
He shelled out his soul and went to God.

As reported by Etheline Taylor

LIFE'S TRADES

It's such a little thing to weep,
So short a thing to sigh;
And yet by trades the size of these
We men and women die!

Emily Dickinson (1830-1886)

WILD CHERRY

Why make your lodging here in this spent lane,
Where but an old man, with his sheep each day,
Twice through the forgotten grass goes by your way,
Half sees you there, and not once looks again?
For you are the very ribs of spring,
And should have many lovers, who have none.
In silver cloaks, in hushed troops down the sun
Should they draw near, oh, strange and lovely thing!
Beauty has no set weather, no sure place;
Her careful pageantries are here as there,
With nothing lost. And soon, some lad may start—
A strayed Mayer in this unremembered space—
At your tall white, and know you very fair,
Let all else go to roof within your heart.

Lizette Woodworth Reese (1856-1935)

GLASS OF CHEER

Drink has drained more blood . . .
Plunged more people into bankruptcy . . .
Slain more children . . .
Dethroned more reason,
Wrecked more manhood,
Dishonored more womanhood . . .
Blasted more lives . . .
Driven more to suicide, and
Dug more graves than any other poisoned scourge
    that ever swept in death-dealing waves
    across the world.

Evangeline Cory Booth (1865-1950)

A lady's imagination is very rapid; it jumps from admiration to love, from love to matrimony in a moment.

Jane Austen (1775-1817)

ACCOMPLISHMENTS

When Aristotle wrote his books,
　　When Milton searched for rhyme,
Did they have toddlers at the knee
　　Requesting dinner time?
When Dante contemplated hell,
　　Or Shakespeare penned a sonnet,
Did Junior interrupt to say
　　His cake had ketchup on it?
When Socrates was teaching youth
　　And Plato wrote the Phaedo,
Were they the ones to clean the mess
　　The children made with Play-doh?
If Edmund Burke had had to work
　　On all his kids' ablutions,
Would he have had the time and strength
　　To speak on revolutions?
Did food get brought when Darwin
　　Sought the origin of species;
Or did he have to hush the tots,
　　And tell them not to tease, please?
When Holmes and Brandeis donned their robes
　　And gave their wise opinions,
Was laundry piled four-feet high
　　With socks mixed up with linens?
How much greater then the task
Of those who manage both,
Who juggle scholarship with child
Development and growth
And how much greater is the praise
For those who persevere,
And finish their advanced degrees
And take up a career!

Elizabeth Ralph Mertz
© Copyright 1975. Reprinted with permission
of *The Radcliffe Quarterly*

INDIAN CHILDREN

Where we walk to school each day
Indian children used to play—
All about our native land,
Where the shops and houses stand.

And the trees were very tall,
And there were no streets at all,
Not a church and not a steeple—
Only woods and Indian people.

Only wigwams on the ground,
And at night bears prowling round—
What a different place to-day
Where we live and work and play!

Annette Wynne, from *For Days and Days*

BOOKS

Books are the carriers of civilization. Without books, history is silent, literature dumb, science crippled, thought and speculation at a standstill. Without books the development of civilization would have been impossible. They are engines of change, windows on the world, "lighthouses" (as a poet said) "erected in the sea of time." They are companions, teachers, magicians, bankers of the treasures of the mind. Books are humanity in print.

Barbara Tuchman (1912-1989)

SELF-DESTRUCT

No witchcraft, no enemy action had silenced the rebirth of life in this stricken world. The people had done it themselves.

Rachel Carson (1907-1964), from *Silent Spring*.
Her lines were applied by an observer to oil spill in Alaska.

TOGETHER

Alone, making my way through the world as best I could,
I found you. We sampled the day's amusements: we walked
in the woods: and we were seen together, holding hands, as
now. We married, I did not intend to give my life away, but
to combine the rest of it in you. I hope I can help you become
what you are. For this is the other half of my becoming.

Note found in a letter from SJS to her husband

DUST

The dust blows up and down
Within the lonely town;
Vague, hurrying, dumb, aloof,
On sill and bow and roof.

What cloudy shapes do fleet
Along the parched street;
Clerks, bishops, kings, go by —
Tomorrow, so shall I!

Lizette Woodworth Reese (1856-1935)

BEGINNING AGAIN

I wish there were some wonderful place
In the land of Beginning Again
Where all our mistakes, and all our heartaches,
And all our error and sin
Could be dropped like a shabby old coat at the door
And never be put on again.

Louise F. Tarkington

FIRST FIG

My candle burns at both ends;
It will not last the night;
But ah, my foes, and oh, my friends,
It gives a lovely light!

Edna St. Vincent Millay (1892-1950)

MEMORIES

Into my heart's treasury
    I slipped a coin
That time cannot take
    Nor a thief purloin
Oh, better than the minting
    Of a gold-crowned king
Is the safe kept memory
    Of a lovely thing

Sarah Teasdale (1884-1933)

SONG OF THANKS

My senses five are five great Cups
    Wherefrom I drink delight!
For them to God a grace I sing
    At morning and at night,
For five fair loving cups are they
    That feed me with delight.

Rachael Annand Taylor

The way to a man's heart is through his stomach.

Fanny Fern [Sara Payson Parton] (1811-1872)

GOSSIP

My name is Gossip. I have no respect for Justice.
I maim without killing, I break hearts and ruin lives.
I am cunning and malicious, and gather strength with age.
The more I am quoted the more I am believed.
I flourish at every level of society.
My victims are helpless. They cannot protect themselves
    against me, because I have no name and no face.
To track me down is impossible. The harder you try, the
    more elusive I become.
I am nobody's friend.
Once I tarnish a reputation it is never quite the same.
I topple governments and wreck marriages.
I ruin careers, cause sleepless nights, heartache, and
    indigestion.
I spawn suspicion and generate grief.
I make innocent people cry in their pillows.
Even my name hisses. I am called Gossip. Office Gossip,
    Shop Gossip, Party Gossip. I make headlines and
    headaches.
Before you repeat a story ask yourself, Is it true? Is it fair?
    Is it necessary? If not—Shut up!

Quoted by Ann Landers

AGREEMENT

Medical men all over the world having merely entered
into a tacit agreement to call all sorts of maladies people are
liable to, in cold weather, by one name; so that one sort of
treatment may serve for all, and their practice be thereby
greatly simplified.

Jane Welsh Carlyle (1801-1866)

WINGS

There is no frigate like a book
   To take us lands away,
Nor any coursers like a page
   Of prancing poetry.

This traverse may the poorest take
   Without oppress of toll;
How frugal is the chariot
   That bears the human soul.

Emily Dickinson (1830-1886)

COURAGE

Riches I hold in light esteem,
And love I laugh to scorn;
And dust of fame was but a dream
That vanished with the morn:

And if I pray, the only prayer
That moves my lips for me
Is, "Leave the heart that now I bear,
And give me liberty!"

Yes, as my swift days near their goal.
'Tis all that I implore—
Through life and death a chainless soul,
With courage to endure.

Emily Bronte (1818-1848)

Women ought to have representatives, instead of being arbitrarily governed without any direct share allowed them in the deliberations of government.

Mary Wollstonecraft [Mary Wollstonecraft Godwin] (1759-1797)

BE QUIET

Be plain in dress, and sober in your diet;
In short, my deary, kiss me and be quiet.

Lady Mary Wortley Montagu (1689-1762)

SOLITUDE

Laugh, and the world laughs with you;
Weep, and you weep alone.
For the sad old earth must borrow its mirth,
But has trouble enough of its own.
Sing, and the hills will answer;
Sigh, it is lost on the air.
The echoes bound to a joyful sound,
But shrink from voicing care.

Rejoice, and men will seek you;
Grieve, and they turn and go.
They want full measure of all your pleasure,
But they do not need your woe.
Be glad, and your friends are many;
Be sad, and you lose them all.
There are none to decline your nectared wine,
But alone you must drink life's gall.

Feast, and your halls are crowded;
Fast, and the world goes by.
Succeed and give, and it helps you live,
But no man can help you die.
There is room in the halls of pleasure
For a long and lordly train,
But one by one we must all file on
Through the narrow aisles of pain.

Ella Wheeler Wilcox (1850-1919)

THE TOUCH OF THE MASTER'S HAND

'Twas battered and scarred, and the auctioneer
Thought it scarcely worth his while
To waste much time on the old violin,
But he held it up with a smile:
"What am I bidden, good folks," he cried,
"Who'll start the bidding for me?"
"A dollar, a dollar;" then, "Two!" "Only two?
Two dollars, and who'll make it three?
Three dollars, once, three dollars, twice;
Going for three—" But no,
From the room, far back, a gray-haired man
Came forward and picked up the bow;
Then, wiping the dust from the old violin,
And tightening the loose strings,
He played a melody pure and sweet
As a caroling angel sings.

The music ceased, and the auctioneer,
With a voice that was quiet and low,
Said: "What am I bid for the old violin?"
And he held it up with the bow.
"A thousand dollars, and who'll make it two?
Two thousand! And who'll make it three?
Three thousand, once, three thousand, twice,
And going, and gone," said he.
The people cheered, but some of them cried,
"We do not quite understand
What changed its worth?" Swift came the reply:
"The touch of the Master's hand."

And many a man with his life out of tune,
And battered and scarred with sin,
Is auctioned cheap to the thoughtless crowd,
Much like the old violin.
A "mess of pottage," a glass of wine;

A game—and he travels on.
He is "going" once, and "going" twice,
He's "going" and almost "gone."
But the Master comes, and the foolish crowd
Never can quite understand
The worth of a soul and the change thats wrought
By the touch of the Master's hand.

Myra Brooks Welch

VELVET SHOES

Let us walk in the white snow
    In a soundless space;
With footsteps quiet and slow,
    At a tranquil pace,
Under veils of white lace.

I shall go shod in silk,
    And you in wool,
White as a white cow's milk,
    More beautiful
Than the breast of a gull.

We shall walk through the still town
    In a windless peace;
We shall step upon white down,
    Upon silver fleece,
    Upon softer than these.

We shall walk in velvet shoes:
    Wherever we go
Silence will fall like dews
    On white silence below.
    We shall walk in the snow.

Elinore Wylie (1885-1928)

WILL POWER

One ship drives east, and another west
With the self-same winds that blow;
'Tis the set of the sails
And not the gales,
Which decides the way to go.

Like the winds of the sea are the ways of fate,
As we voyage along through life;
'Tis the will of the soul
That decides the goal,
And not the calm or the strife.

Ella Wheeler Wilcox (1850-1919)

BIRTHDAY

My heart is like a singing bird
   Whose nest is a watered shoot;
My heart is like an apple tree
   Whose boughs are bent with thick-set fruit;
My heart is like a rainbow shell
   That paddles in a halcyon sea;
My heart is gladder than all these
   Because my love is come to me.

Raise me a dais of silk and down;
   Hang it with vair and purple dyes;
Carve it in doves and pomegranates,
   And peacocks with a hundred eyes;
Work it in gold and silver grapes,
   In leaves and silver fleur-de-lys;
Because the birthday of my life
   Is come, my love is come to me.

Christina Rossetti (1830-1894)

DREAMS

Hold fast your dreams!
Within your heart
Keep one still, secret spot
Where dreams may go,
And sheltered so,
May thrive and grow
Where doubt and fear are not.
O keep a place apart,
Within your heart,
For little dreams to go!

Think still of lovely things that are not true.
Let wish and magic work at will in you.
Be sometimes blind to sorrow. Make believe!
Forget the calm that lies
In disillusioned eyes.
Though we all know that we must die,
Yet you and I
May walk like gods and be
Even now at home in immortality.

We see so many ugly things—
Deceits and wrongs and quarrelings;
We know, alas! we know
How quickly fade
The color in the west,
The bloom upon the flower,
The bloom upon the breast
And youth's blind hour.
Yet keep within your heart,
A place apart
Where little dreams may go,
May thrive and grow.
Hold fast—hold fast your dreams!

Louise Driscoll (1875-1960)

DANDELION

O little Soldier with the golden helmet,
What are you guarding on my lawn?
You with your green gun
And your yellow beard,
Why do you stand so stiff?
There is only the grass to fight!

Hilda Conkling, written at age eight

OLDER

Let me grow lovely, growing old—
    So many fine things do;
Laces and ivory, and gold,
    And silks need not be new;

And there is healing in old trees,
    Old streets a glamour hold;
Why may not I, as well as these'
    Grow lovely, growing old?

Karle Wilson Baker

COLORS

You cannot choose your battlefield,
The gods do that for you,
But you can plant a standard
Where a standard never flew.

Nathalia Crane (1913-   )

WATCHING

She always leaned to watch us,
　Anxious if we were late,
In winter by the window,
　In summer by the gate;

And though we mocked her tenderly,
　Who had such foolish care,
The long way home would seem more safe
　Because she waited there.

Her thoughts were all so full of us,
　She never could forget!
And so I think that where she is
　She must be watching yet,

Waiting till we come home to her,
　Anxious if we are late—
Watching from Heaven's window,
　Leaning from Heaven's gate.

Margaret Widdemer (1880-　)

LIFE

You and I picked up Life and looked at it curiously;
We did not know whether to keep it for a plaything or not.
It was beautiful to see, like a red firecracker,
And we knew too that it was lighted.
We dropped it while the fuse was still burning.

Mary Carolyn Davies (1888-　)

MEN

I like men.
   They stride about,
They reach in their pockets
   And pull things out;

They look important,
   They rock on their toes,
They lose all their buttons
   Off their clothes;

They throw away pipes,
   They find them again.
Men are queer creatures;
   I like men.

Dorothy E. Reid

FUTILITY SINGS

Pretty futility
Always declares
There's nothing so good
As a basket of pears,

Nothing so tranquil,
Nothing so sweet,
As eating ripe pears
In the quiet of heat.

She straightens her ruffles,
She smiles as she swings,
And when she has eaten
Futility sings.

Elizabeth Coatsworth (1893-   )

SOULS

My soul goes clad in gorgeous things,
Scarlet and gold and blue.
And at her shoulder sudden wings
Like long flames flicker through.

And she is swallow-fleet, and free
From mortal bonds and bars.
She laughs, because eternity
Blossoms for her with stars!

O folk who scorn my stiff gray gown,
My dull and foolish face,
Can ye not see my soul flash down,
A singing flame through space?

And folk whose earth-stained looks I hate,
Why may I not divine
Your souls, that must be passionate,
Shining and swift, as mine?

Fannie Sterns Davis (1884-   )

MARIGOLD GARDEN

In the pleasant green Garden
    We sat down to tea;
"Do you take sugar?" and
    "Do you take milk?"
She'd got a new gown on—
    A smart one of silk.
We all were as happy
    As happy could be,
On that bright Summer's day
    When she asked us to tea.

Kate Greenaway (1846-1901), from *Marigold Garden*

Since trifles make the sum of human things,
And half our misery from our foibles springs.

Hannah More (1745-1833)

WASTE

There's hardly anything so small,
    So trifling or so mean,
That we may never want at all,
    For service unforeseen;
And wilful waste, depend upon't,
Brings almost always, woeful want!

Jane Taylor (1783-1824)

THE RAINS OF SPRING

The rains of spring
Which hang to the branches
    Of the green willow,
Look like pearls upon a string.

Lady Ise, from *Little Pictures of Japan*

ME

Alone I walked the ocean strand;
A pearly shell was in my hand;
I stooped and wrote upon the sand
My name—the year—the day—.

Hannah Flagg Gould (1789-1865), from "A Name On The Sand"

EXPERIENCE

Deborah danced, when she was two,
As buttercups and daffodils do;
Spirited, frail, naively bold,
Her hair a ruffled crest of gold,
And whenever she spoke her voice went singing
Like water from a mountain springing.

But now her step is quiet and slow;
She walks the way primroses go;
Her hair is yellow instead of gilt,
Her voice is losing its lovely lilt,
And in place of her wild, delightful ways
A quaint precision rules her days.

For Deborah now is three, and oh,
She knows so much that she did not know.

Aline (Mrs. Joyce) Kilmer (1888-1941)

Would you be young again?
So would not I—
One tear to memory given,
Onward I'd hie.

Caroline Oliphant, Lady Nairne (1766-1845)

The distance is nothing; it is only the first step which counts.

Madame Du Deffand (1697-1784)

FORTUNE

I've seen the smiling
Of fortune beguiling,
I've felt all her favors and found her decay;
Sweet was her blessing,
Kind her caressing:
But now they are fled, are fled far away.

Alicia Rutherford Cockburn (1712-1794)

GOSSIP

To all the gossip that I hear
I'll give no faith; to what I see
But only half, for it is clear
All that led up is dark to me.
Learn we the larger life to live,
To comprehend is to forgive.

Henrietta A. Huxley (1825-1914)
"Tout Comprendre, C'est Tout Pardonner"

SOMEONE'S MAN

It is a truth universally acknowledged, that a single man in possession of a good fortune, must be in want of a wife.

However little known the feelings or views of such a man may be on his first entering a neighbourhood, this truth is so well fixed in the minds of the surrounding families, that he is considered as the rightful property of some one or other of their daughters.

Jane Austen (1775-1817)

DARK FOUNTAIN

To evil habit's earliest wile
Lend neither ear, nor glance, nor smile—
Choke the dark fountain ere it flows,
Nor e'en admit the camel's nose.

Lydia Huntley Sigourney (1791-1865), from "The Camel's Nose"

To bear, to nurse, to rear,
To watch and then to lose,
To see my bright ones disappear,
Drawn up like morning dews.

Jean Ingelow (1820-1897)

NOVELS

"Only a novel" . . . in short, only some work in which the greatest powers of the mind are displayed, in which the most thorough knowledge of human nature, the happiest delineation of its varieties, the liveliest effusions of wit and humor are conveyed to the world in the best chosen language.

Jane Austen (1775-1817)

PARTING

Hast thou forgotten how soon we must sever?
Oh! hast thou forgotten this day we must part?
It may be for years, and it may be forever:
Then why art thou silent, thou voice of my heart?

Julia Crawford (1800-1885)

PLANT A TREE

He who plants a tree
    Plants a hope.
    Rootlets up through fibres blindly grope;
Leaves unfold into horizons free.
    So man's life must climb
    From the clods of time
    Unto heavens sublime.
Canst thou prophesy, thou little tree,
What the glory of thy boughs shall be?

He who plants a tree
    Plants a joy;
    Plants a comfort that will never cloy;
Every day a fresh reality,
    Beautiful and strong,
    To whose shelter throng
    Creatures blithe with song.
If thou canst but know, thou happy tree,
Of the bliss that shall inhabit thee!

He who plants a tree,—
    He plants peace.
    Under its green curtains jargons cease.
Leaf and zephyr murmur soothingly;
    Shadows soft with sleep
    Down tired eyelids creep,
    Balm of slumber deep.
Never hast thou dreamed, thou blessed tree,
Of the benediction thou shalt be.

He who plants a tree,—
    He plants a youth;
    Vigor won for centuries in sooth;
Life of time, that hints eternity!
    Boughs their strength uprear:

New shoots every year,
    On old shoots appear;
Thou shalt teach the ages, sturdy tree,
Youth of soul is immortality.

He who plants a tree,—
    He plants love,
    Tents of coolness spreading out above
Wayfarers he may not live to see.
    Gifts that grow are best;
    Hands that bless are best;
    Plant! life does the rest!
Heaven and earth helps him who plants a tree,
And his work its own reward shall be.

                                        Lucy Larcom (1824-1893)

TRUTH

Truth is the nursing mother of genius. No man can be absolutely true to himself, eschewing cant, compromise, servile imitation, and complaisance, without becoming original for there is in every creature a fountain of life which, if not choked back by stones and other dead rubbish, will create a fresh atmosphere, and bring to life fresh beauty.

                                  Margaret Fuller (Ossoli) (1810-1850)

MIND'S EYE

It lies around us like a cloud,
    A world we do not see;
Yet the sweet closing of an eye
    May bring us there to be.

                                Harriet Beecher Stowe (1811-1896)

NOBILITY

True worth is in being, not seeming,—
    In doing, each day that goes by,
Some little good—not in dreaming
    Of great things to do by and by.
For whatever men say in their blindness,
    And spite of the fancies of youth,
There's nothing so kingly as kindness,
    And nothing so royal as truth.

We get back our mete as we measure—
    We cannot do wrong and feel right,
Nor can we give pain and feel pleasure,
    For justice avenges each slight.
The air for the wing of the sparrow,
    The bush for the robin and wren,
But always the path that is narrow
    And straight, for the children of men.

'Tis not in the pages of story
    The heart of its ills to beguile,
Though he who makes courtship to glory
    Gives all that he has for her smile.
For when from her heights he has won her,
    Alas! it is only to prove
That nothing's so sacred as honor,
    And nothing so loyal as love!

We cannot make bargains for blisses,
    Nor catch them like fishes in nets;
And sometimes the thing our life misses
    Helps more than the thing that it gets.
For good lieth not in pursuing,
    Nor gaining of great nor of small,
But just in the doing, and doing
    As we would be done by, is all.

Through envy, through malice, through hating,
  Against the world early and late,
No jot of our courage abating—
  Our part is to work and to wait.
And slight is the sting of his trouble
  Whose winnings are less than his worth;
For he who is honest is noble,
  Whatever his fortunes or birth.

Alice Cary (1820-1871)

THE MINUET

Grandma told me all about it,
Told me so I couldn't doubt it,
How she danced, my grandma danced; long ago—
How she held her pretty head,
How her dainty skirt she spread,
How she slowly leaned and rose—long ago.

Grandma's hair was bright and sunny,
Dimpled cheeks too, oh, how funny!
Really quite a pretty girl—long ago.
Bless her! why, she wears a cap,
Grandma does, and takes a nap
Every single day: and yet
Grandma danced the minuet—long ago.

"Modern ways are quite alarming,"
Grandma says, "but boys were charming"
(Girls and boys she means, of course) "long ago."
Brave but modest, grandly shy;
She would like to have us try
Just to feel like those who met
In the graceful minuet—long ago.

Mary Mapes Dodge (1838-1905), from "Along the Way"

MEN

You men have difficulties, and privations, and dangers enough to struggle with. You are always laboring and toiling, exposed to every risk and hardship. Your home, country, friends, all quitted. Neither time, nor health, nor life, to be called your own. It would be too hard, indeed . . . if woman's feelings were to be added to all this.

Jane Austen (1775-1817), from Persuasion

TO LOVE

Unless you can muse in a crowd all day
On the absent face that fixed you;
Unless you can love, as the angels may,
With the breadth of heaven betwixt you;
Unless you can dream that his faith is fast,
Through behoving and unbehoving;
Unless you can die when the dream is past—
Oh, never call it loving!

Elizabeth Barrett Browning (1806-1861), from "A Woman's Shortcomings"

SECRETS

Under thy hooded mantle I can see
Thy wavelets of soft hair, like those that lie
On a girl's forehead; and thy unlined brow,
Pregnant with thought inbreathed, betrayeth not
One of thy secrets saving this alone,—
That thou hast loved and suffered.

Julia Caroline Ripley Dorr (1825-1913), from "In Rock Creek Cemetery"

ESCAPE

Eliza made her desperate retreat across the river just in the dusk of twilight. The grey mist of evening, rising slowly from the river, enveloped her as she disappeared up the bank, and the swollen current and floundering masses of ice presented a hopeless barrier between her and her pursuer.

Harriet Beecher Stowe (1811-1896)

GENTLEMEN

Whom do we dub as Gentlemen? The
knave, the fool, the brute —
If they but own full tithe of gold, and
wear a courtly suit.

Eliza Cook (1818-1889)

BRIGHT DAYS

Sleep not, dream not; this bright day
Will not, cannot last for aye;
Bliss like thine is bought by years
Dark with torment and with tears.

Charlotte Bronte (1818-1848), from "Sleep Not"

WORK

Work and your house shall be duly fed:
Work, and rest shall be won;
I hold that man had better be dead
Than alive when work is done.

Alice Cary (1820-1871), from "Work"

I SHALL NOT PASS THIS WAY AGAIN
A Symphony

I shall not pass this way again—
  Although it bordered be with flowers.
  Although I rest in fragrant bowers,
    And hear the singing
    Of song-birds winging
To highest heaven their gladsome flight;
Though moons are full and stars are bright,
And winds and waves are softly sighing,
While leafy trees make low replying;
Though voices clear in joyous strain
Repeat a jubilant refrain;
Though rising suns their radiance throw
On summer's green and winter's snow,
In such rare splendor that my heart
Would ache from scenes like these to part;
  Though beauties heighten,
  And life-lights brighten,
And joys proceed from every pain,—
I shall not pass this way again.

Then let me pluck the flowers that blow,
And let me listen as I go
  To music rare
  That fills the air;
  And let hereafter
  Songs and laughter
Fill every pause along the way;
And to my spirit let me say:
"O soul, be happy; soon 'tis trod,
The path made thus for thee by God.
Be happy, thou, and bless His name
By whom such marvelous beauty came."
And let no chance by me be lost

To kindness show at any cost.
I shall not pass this way again;
Then let me now relieve some pain,
Remove some barrier from the road,
Or brighten someone's heavy load;
A helping hand to this one lend,
Then turn some other to befriend.

O God, forgive
That now I live
As if I might, sometime, return
To bless the weary ones that yearn
For help and comfort every day, —
For there be such along the way.
O God, forgive that I have seen
The beauty only, have not been
Awake to sorrow such as this;
That I have drunk the cup of bliss
Remembering not that those there be
Who drink the dregs of misery.

I love the beauty of the scene,
Would roam again o'er fields so green;
But since I may not, let me spend
My strength for others to the end, —
For those who tread on rock and stone,
And bear their burdens all alone,
Who loiter not in leafy bowers,
Nor hear the birds nor pluck the flowers.
A larger kindness give to me,
A deeper love and sympathy;
Then, O, one day
May someone say —
Remembering a lessened pain —
"Would she could pass this way again."

Eva Rose York (1858-   )

GENIUS

Genius hath electric power
Which earth can never tame,
Bright suns may scorch and dark clouds lower,
Its flash is still the same.

Lydia Maria Child (1802-1880)

LOVE NOT

Love not! Love not! Ye hapless sons of clay;
Hope's gayest wreaths are made of earthly flowers —
Things that are made to fade and fall away,
Ere they have blossomed for a few short hours.

Caroline Elizabeth Sheridan Norton, Lady Maxwell (1808-1877)

SLEEP

Of all the thoughts of God that are
Borne inward into souls afar,
Along the psalmist's music deep,
Now tell me if that any is,
For gift or grace, surpassing this:
"He giveth his beloved—sleep"

Elizabeth Barrett Browning 1806-1861)

Oh, my son's my son till he gets him a wife,
But my daughter's my daughter all her life.

Dinah Maria Mulock Craik (1826-1887)

LISTENERS

Man dwells apart, though not alone,
He walks among his peers unread;
The best of thoughts which he hath known
For lack of listeners are not said.

Jean Ingelow (1820-1897), from "Afterthought"

PRIVILEGE

Knowing, as I well do, that the privilege of motherhood is God granted, how can I possibly provide any other than the fullest degree of humility, commitment and responsibility to that child in providing it the best of life as part of that privilege?

Jeneal White

DREAMS

Sometimes I think the things we see
Are shadows of the things to be;
That what we plan we build;
That every hope that hath been crossed,
In heaven shall be fulfilled.

Phoebe Cary (1824-1874), from "Dreams and Realities"

GIVING

Love that asketh love again
Finds the barter nought but pain;
Love that giveth in full store
Aye receives as much, and more.

Dinah Maria Muloch Craik (1826-1887)

THE SPIDER AND THE FLY
A Fable

"Will you walk into my parlor?" said the spider to the fly;
"'Tis the prettiest little parlor that ever you did spy.
The way into my parlor is up a winding stair,
And I have many pretty things to show when you are there."
"Oh no, no," said the little fly, "to ask me is in vain,
For who goes up your winding stair can ne'er come down
     again."

"I'm sure you must be weary, dear, with soaring up so high;
Will you rest upon my little bed?" said the spider to the fly.
"There are pretty curtains drawn around, the sheets are fine
     and thin,
And if you'd like to rest awhile, I'll snugly tuck you in."
"O no, no," said the little fly, "for I've often heard it said,
They never, never wake again, who sleep upon your bed."

Said the cunning spider to the fly, "Dear friend, what shall
     I do?
To prove the warm affection I've always felt for you?
I have within my pantry good store of all that's nice;
I'm sure you're very welcome; will you please to take a slice?"
"O no, no," said the little fly, "kind sir, that cannot be;
I've heard what's in your pantry, and I do not wish to see."

"Sweet creature!" said the spider, "you're witty and you're
     wise,
How handsome are your gauzy wings, how brilliant are your
     eyes!
I have a little looking glass upon my parlor shelf,
If you'll step in one moment, dear, you shall behold
     yourself."
"I thank you, gentle sir," she said, "for what you're pleased
     to say,
And bidding you good-morning now, I'll call another day."

The spider turned him round about, and went into his den,
For well he knew the silly fly would soon be back again:
So he wove a subtle web, in a little corner sly,
And set his table ready to dine upon the fly.
Then he came out to his door again, and merrily did sing,
"Come hither, hither, pretty fly, with the pearl and silver
    wing:
Your robes are green and purple; there's a crest upon your
    head;
Your eyes are like the diamond bright, but mine are dull as
    lead."

Alas, alas! how very soon this silly little fly,
Hearing his wily flattering words, came slowly flitting by.
With buzzing wings she hung aloft, then near and nearer
    drew,
Thinking only of her brilliant eyes, and green and purple
    hue;
Thinking only of her crested head—poor foolish thing! At
    last,
Up jumped the cunning spider, and fiercely held her fast.
He dragged her up his winding stair, into his dismal den,
Within his little parlor; but she ne'er came out again!

And now dear little children, who may this story read,
To idle, silly, flattering words, I pray you ne'er give
    heed;
Unto an evil counselor close heart, and ear, and eye,
And take a lesson from this tale of the Spider and the Fly.

                                    Mary Howitt (1799-1888)

In my end is my beginning.

            Motto of Mary Stuart, Queen of Scots (1542-1587)

We are not interested in the possibility of defeat.

            Victoria, Queen of Great Britain (1819-1901)

THOREAU

For such as he there is no death;—
His life the eternal life commands;
Above man's aims his nature rose.
The wisdom of a just content
Made one small spot a continent
And turned to poetry Life's prose.

Louisa May Alcott (1832-1888)

ENDURANCE

Behold, we live through all things—famine, thirst,
Bereavement, pain; sorrow; all grief and misery,
All woe and sorrow; life inflicts its worst
On soul and body—but we cannot die,
Though we be sick, and tired, and faint, and worn,—
Lo, all things can be borne!

Elizabeth Akers Allen (1832-1911)

DEATH AT SEA

God bless them all who die at sea!
If they must sleep in restless waves,
God makes them dream they are ashore,
With grass above their graves.

Sarah Orne Jewett (1849-1909)

Happiness is not a station you arrive at, but a manner of traveling.

Margaret Lee Runbeck

THANKSGIVING DAY

Over the river and through the wood,
　To grandfather's house we go;
　　The horse knows the way
　　To carry the sleigh
　Through the white and drifted snow.

Over the river and through the wood—
　Oh, how the wind does blow!
　　It stings the toes
　　And bites the nose,
　As over the ground we go.

Over the river and through the wood,
　To have a first-rate play.
　　Hear the bells ring,
　　"Ting-a-ling-ding!"
　Hurrah for Thanksgiving Day!

Over the river and through the wood
　Trot fast, my dapple-gray!
　　Spring over the ground,
　　Like a hunting hound!
　For this is Thanksgiving Day.

Over the river and through the wood,
　And straight through the barnyard gate.
　　We seem to go
　　Extremely slow,—
　It is so hard to wait!

Over the river and through the wood—
　Now grandmother's cap I spy!
　　Hurrah for the fun!
　　Is the pudding done?
　Hurrah for the pumpkin-pie!

Lydia Maria Child (1802-1880)

COUNTRY SUMMER

Now the rich cherry whose sleek wood
And top with silver petals traced,
Like a strict box its gems encased,
Has spilt from out that cunning lid,
All in an innocent green round,
Those melting rubies which it hid;
With moss ripe-strawberry-encrusted,
So birds get half, and minds lapse merry
To taste that deep-red, lark's-bite berry,
And blackcap-bloom is yellow-dusted.

The wren that thieved it in the eaves
A trailer of the rose could catch
To her poor droopy sloven thatch,
And side by side with the wren's brood—
O lovely time of beggars' luck—
Opens the quaint and hairy bud;
And full and golden is the yield
Of cows that never have to house,
But all night nibble under boughs,
Or cool their sides in the moist field.

Into the rooms flow meadow airs,
The warm farm-baking smell blows round;
Inside and out, and sky and ground
Are much the same; the wishing star,
Hesperus, kind and early-born,
Is risen only finger-far.
All stars stand close in summer air,
And tremble, and look mild as amber;
When wicks are lighted in the chamber
You might say stars were settling there.

Now straightening from the flowery hay,
Down the still light the mowers look;
Or turn, because their dreaming shook,

And they waked half to other days,
When left alone in yellow-stubble
The rusty-coated mare would graze.
Yet thick the lazy dreams are born,
Another thought can come to mind,
But like the shivering of the wind,
Morning and Evening in the corn.

Leonie Adams (1899-   )

GREEN THINGS GROWING

O the green things growing, the green things growing,
The faint sweet smell of the green things growing!
I should like to live, whether I smile or grieve,
Just to watch the happy life of my green things growing.

O the fluttering and the pattering of those green things
    growing!
How they talk each to each, when none of us are knowing;
In the wonderful white of the weird moonlight
Or the dim dreamy dawn when the cocks are crowing.

I love, I love them so—my green things growing!
And I think that they love me, without false showing;
For by many a tender touch, they comfort me so much,
With the soft mute comfort of green things growing.

And in the rich store of their blossoms glowing
Ten for one I take they're on me bestowing:
Oh, I should like to see, if God's will it may be,
Many, many a summer of my green things growing!

But if I must be gathered for the angel's sowing,
Sleep out of sight awhile, like the green things growing,
Though dust to dust return, I think I'll scarcely mourn,
If I may change into green things growing.

Dinah Maria Mulock Craik (1826-1887)

HOW TO TELL THE WILD ANIMALS

If ever you should go by chance
    To jungles in the East;
And if there should to you advance
    A large and tawny beast,
If he roars at you as you're dyin'
You'll know it is the Asian Lion.

Or if some time when roaming round,
    A noble wild beast greets you,
With black stripes on a yellow ground,
    Just notice if he eats you.
This simple rule may help you learn
The Bengal Tiger to discern.

If strolling forth, a beast you view,
    Whose hide with spots is peppered,
As soon as he has lept on you,
    You'll know it is the Leopard.
'Twill do no good to roar with pain,
He'll only lep and lep again.

If when you're walking round your yard,
    You meet a creature there,
Who hugs you very, very hard,
    Be sure it is the Bear.
If you have any doubt, I guess
He'll give you just one more caress.

Though to distinguish beasts of prey
    A novice might nonplus,
The Crocodiles you always may
    Tell from Hyenas thus:
Hyenas come with merry smiles;
But if they weep, they're Crocodiles.

The true Chameleon is small,
    A lizard sort of thing;
He hasn't any ears at all,
    And not a single wing.
If there is nothing in the tree,
'Tis the Chameleon you see.

Carolyn Wells (1869-1942)

LITTLE THINGS

Little drops of water,
    Little grains of sand,
Make the mighty ocean
    And the pleasant land.

Thus the little minutes,
    Humble though they be,
Make the mighty ages
    Of eternity.

Julia A. Fletcher Carney (1823-1908)

TURN BACK

Backward, turn backward, O Time, in your flight,
    Make me a child again just for tonight!
Mother, come back from the echoless shore,
    Take me again to your heart, as of yore;
Kiss from my forehead the furrows of care,
    Smooth the few silver threads out of my hair;
Over my slumbers your loving watch keep,
    Rock me to sleep, Mother, rock me to sleep.

Elizabeth Akers Allen (1832-1911)

GOD KNOWS

The land enclosed within the fence
    To me seemed very great.
I passed that way from day to day.
    A man who stood by the gate
      Who owned the land.

His hair was gray and he was bent
    By years of heavy toil.
"This land," he said, "was my homestead
    And I improved the soil.
      I own the land."

The years passed by; again I chanced
    To pass along the road.
I saw a face I could not place;
    And yet it plainly showed
      He owned the land.

A son perhaps of him I knew;
    At least I would find out,
Before going on where he had gone;
    Who once was there about,
      And owned the land.

The young man took me to a plot
    Where his body lay at rest
From all his toil, improving soil.
    Oh, surely God knows best
      Who owns the land.

Hannah C. Ashby

Diamonds are only chunks of coal,
That stuck to their jobs, you see.

Minnie Richard Smith

THE STAR

Twinkle, twinkle, little star,
How I wonder what you are!
Up above the world so high,
Like a diamond in the sky.

When the blazing sun is set,
When the grass with dew is wet,
Then you show your little light,
Twinkle, twinkle, all the night.

Then the traveler in the dark,
Thanks you for your tiny spark;
He could not see which way to go
If you did not twinkle so.

In the dark blue sky you keep,
And often through my curtains peep,
For you never shut your eye
Till the sun is in the sky.

As your bright and shiny spark,
Lights the traveler in the dark,
Though I know not what you are,
Twinkle, twinkle, little star.

Jane Taylor (1783-1824), from "Rhymes for the Nursery"

GOOD AND BAD

Every home is perforce a good or bad educational center. It does its work in spite of every effort to shrink or supplement it. No teacher can entirely undo what it does, be that good or bad.

Ida Tarbell (1857-1944)

Marriage should be something worked toward with every step you take. It shouldn't be an unforeseen emergency, like being called upon unexpectedly to make a speech on a subject you've never heard of.

Margaret Lee Runbeck

A young man was once asked . . . why he did not . . . marry a certain very beautiful but rather frivolous girl. . . . "Is she a person whom you would pick out to entrust with the bringing up of your children?" he said. When his questioners conceded this was not so, he added, "Well, I do not choose to entrust her with the bringing up of mine."

Alice Stone Blackwell

PEACE

I came at morn; 'twas spring, I smiled,
    The fields with green were clad;
I walked abroad at noon, and lo!
    'Twas summer—I was glad;
I sate me down; 'twas autumn eve,
    And I with sadness wept;
I laid me down at night, and then
    'Twas winter, and I slept.

Mary Pyper

I have to thank God I'm a woman,
For in these ordered days a woman only
Is free to be very hungry, very lonely

Anna Wickham (1884-   )

CALM ON THE BOSOM OF THY GOD

Calm on the bosom of thy God,
    Young spirit! rest thee now.
Even while with us thy footstep trod,
    His seal was on thy brow.

Dust, to its narrow house beneath!
    Soul, to its place on high! —
They that have seen thy look in death
    No more may fear to die.

Lone are the paths, and sad the bowers,
    Whence thy meek smile is gone;
But O, a brighter home than ours
    In heaven is now thine own!

Felicia Dorothea Hemans

SINCERE

To be sincere with ourselves is better and harder than to be painstakingly accurate with others.

Agnes Repplier (1855-1950)

ROCK ME TO SLEEP

Backward, turn backward, O Time, in your flight,
Make me a child again just for to-night!
Mother come back from the echoless shore,
Take me again to your heart as of yore;
Kiss from my forehead the furrows of care,
Smooth the few silver threads out of my hair;
Over my slumbers your loving watch keep; —
Rock me to sleep, mother, — rock me to sleep!

Excerpt from "Rock Me to Sleep," Florence Percy (1832-1911)

THEY SAY

Have you heard of the terrible family They,
And the dreadful venomous things They say?
Why, half the gossip under the sun,
If you trace it back, you will find begun
    In that wretched House of They.
A numerous family, so I am told,
And its genealogical tree is old;
For ever since Adam and Eve began
To build up the curious race of man,
    Has existed the House of They.
Gossip-mongers and spreaders of lies,
Horrid people whom all despise!
And yet the best of us now and then,
Repeat queer tales about women and men
    And quote the House of They.
They live like lords, and never labor;
A They's one task is to watch his neighbor,
And tell his business and private affairs
To the world at large; they are sowers of tares—
    These folks in the House of They.
It is wholly useless to follow a They
With a whip or a gun, for he slips away
And into his house, where you cannot go;
It is locked and bolted and guarded so—
    This horrible House of They.
Though you cannot get in, yet they get out,
And spread their villainous tales about;
Of all the rascals under the sun
Who have come to punishment, never one
    Belonged to the House of They.

Ella Wheeler Wilcox (1850-1919)

Life is the totality of those functions which resist death.

Marie Francois Xavier Bichat (1771-1802)

A NARROW FELLOW IN THE GRASS
(The Snake)

A narrow fellow in the grass
Occasionally rides;
You may have met him,—did you not?
His notice sudden is.

The grass divides as with a comb,
A spotted shaft is seen;
And then it closes at your feet
And opens further on.

He likes a boggy acre,
A floor to cool for corn.
Yet when a child, and barefoot,
I more than once, at morn,

Have passed, I thought, a whiplash
Unbraiding in the sun,—
When, stooping to secure it,
It wrinkled, and was gone.

Several of nature's people
I know, and they know me;
I feel for them a transport
Of cordiality;

But never met this fellow,
Attended or alone,
Without a tighter breathing,
And zero at the bone.

Emily Dickinson (1830-1886)

Love is the whole history of a woman's life, it is but an episode in a man's.

Madame de Staël [Germaine, Baronne de Staël-Holstein] (1766-1817)

WORDS

A word is dead
When it is said,
  Some say.
I say it just
Begins to live
  That day.

Emily Dickinson (1830-1886)

SUNDOWN

This is the time lean woods shall spend
A steeped-up twilight, and the pale evening drink,
And the perilous roe, the leaper to the west brink,
Trembling and bright, to the caverned cloud descend.

Now shall you see pent oak gone gusty and frantic,
Stooped with dry weeping, ruinously unloosing
The sparse disheveled leaf, or reared and tossing
A dreary scarecrow bough in funeral antic

Aye, tatter you and rend,
Oak heart, to your profession mourning; not obscure
The outcome, not crepuscular; on the deep floor,
Sable and gold match lusters and contend.

And rags of shrouding will not muffle the slain.
This is the immortal extinction, the priceless wound
Not to be staunched. The live gold leaks beyond,
And matter's sanctified, dipped in a gold stain.

Leonie Adams (1899-   )

3

LIFE
AND LIVING

GIVING

Give plenty of what is given to you,
And listen to pity's call;
Don't think the little you give is great
And the much you get is small.

Phoebe Cary (1824-1874)

HAPPY LIFE

Three ounces are necessary, first of Patience,
Then, of Repose & Peace; of Conscience
A pound entire is needful;
of Pastimes of all sorts, too,
Should be gathered as much as the hand can hold;
Of Pleasant Memory & of Hope three good drachms
There must be at least. But they should moistened be
With a liquor made from True Pleasures which rejoice the
    heart. Then of Love's
Magic Drops, a few—
But use them sparingly, for they may bring a flame
Which naught but tears can drown,
Grind the whole and mix therewith of Merriment, an
    ounce
To even. Yet all this may not bring happiness
Except in your Orisons you lift your voice
To Him who holds the gift of health.

Margaret of Navarre (1492-1549)

SONG

I make my shroud, but no one knows—
So shimmering fine it is and fair,
With stitches set in even rows.
I make my shroud and no one knows.

In door-way where the lilac blows,
Humming a little wandering air,
I make my shroud and no one knows,
So shimmering fine it is and fair.

Adelaide Crapsey (1878-1914)

LAST DAYS

As one who follows a departing friend,
Destined to cross the great dividing sea,
I watch and follow these departing days,
That go so grandly, lifting up their crowns
Still regal, though their victor Autumn comes.
Gifts they bestow, which I accept, return,
As gifts exchanged between a loving pair,
Who may possess them as memorials
Of pleasures ended by the shadow—Death.
What matter which shall vanish hence, if both
Are transitory—me, and these bright hours—
And of the future ignorant alike?
From all our social thralls I would be free.
Let care go down the wind—as hounds afar,
Within their kennels baying unseen foes,
Give to calm sleepers only calmer dreams.
Here will I rest alone: the morning mist
Conceals no form but mine; the evening dew
Freshens but faded flowers and my worn face.
When the noon basks among the wooded hills
I too will bask, as silent as the air
So thick with sun-motes, dyed like yellow gold,
Or colored purple like an unplucked plum.
The thrush, now lonesome, for her young have
flown,
May flutter her brown wings across my path;
And creatures of the sod with brilliant eyes
May leap beside me, and familiar grow.
The moon shall rise among her floating clouds,
Black, vaporous fans, and crinkled globes of pearl,
And her sweet silver light be given to me.
To watch and follow these departing days
Must be my choice; and let me mated be

With Solitude; may memory and hope
Unite to give me faith that nothing dies;
To show me always, what I pray to know,
That man alone may speak the word—Farewell.

Elizabeth Stoddard (1823-1902)

LIFE

Life, believe, is not a dream
So dark as sages say;
Oft a little morning rain
Foretells a pleasant day.

Charlotte Bronte (1816-1855), from "Life"

HIC JACET

(preceding a name on a tombstone)

So love is dead that has been quick so long!
Close, then, his eyes, and bear him to his rest,
With eglantine and myrtle on his breast,
And leave him there, their pleasant scents among;
And chant a sweet and melancholy song
About the charms whereof he was possessed,
And how of all things he was loveliest,
And to compare with aught were him to wrong.
Leave him beneath the still and solemn stars,
That gather and look down from their far place
With their long calm our brief woes to deride,
Until the Sun the Morning's gate unbars
And mocks, in turn, our sorrows with his face;—
And yet, had Love been Love, he had not died.

Louise Chandler Moulton (1835-1908)

DEATH

Because I could not stop for Death,
He kindly stopped for me;
The carriage held but just ourselves
And Immortality.

We slowly drove, he knew no haste,
And I had put away
My labor, and my leisure too,
For his civility.

We passed the school where children played
At wrestling in a ring;
We passed the fields of gazing grain,
We passed the setting sun.

We paused before a house that seemed
A swelling of the ground;
The roof was scarcely visible,
The cornice but a mound.

Since then 'tis centuries; but each
Feels shorter than the day
I first surmised the horses' heads
Were toward eternity.

Emily Dickinson (1830-1886), from "Complete Poems" VIII

SUSANNA AND THE ELDERS

"Why do
You thus devise
Evil against her?" "For that
She is beautiful, delicate;
Therefore."

Adelaide Crapsey (1878-1914)

VENUS OF THE LOUVRE

Down the long hall she glistens like a star,
The foam-born mother of Love, transfixed to stone,
Yet none the less immortal, breathing on.
Time's brutal hand hath maimed but could not mar,
When first the enthralled enchantress from afar
Dazzled mine eyes, I saw her not alone,
Serenely poised on her world-worshipped throne,
As when she guided once her doze-drawn car,—
But at her feet a pale, death-stricken Jew,
Her life adorer, sobbed farewell to love.
Here Heine wept! Here still he weeps anew,
Nor ever shall his shadow lift or move,
While mourns one ardent heart, one poet-brain,
For vanished Hellas and Hebraic pain.

Emma Lazarus (1849-1887)

NO ESCAPE

Since there is no escape, since at the end
    My body will be utterly destroyed,
This hand I love as I have loved a friend,
    This body I tended, wept with and enjoyed;
Since there is no escape even for me
    Who love life with a love too sharp to bear:
The scent of orchards in the rain, the sea
    And hours alone too still and sure for prayer—
Since darkness waits for me, then all the more
Let me go down as waves sweep to the shore
    In pride, and let me sing with my last breath;
In these few hours of light I lift my head;
Life is my lover—I shall leave the dead
    If there is any way to baffle death.

Sara Teasdale (1884-1933)

MONOCHROME

Shut fast again in beauty's sheath
Where ancient forms renew,
The round world seems above, beneath,
One wash of faintest blue,

And air and tide so stilly sweet
In nameless union lie,
The little far off fishing fleet
Goes drifting up the sky.

Secure of neither misted coast
Nor ocean undefined,
Our flagging sail is like the ghost
Of one that served mankind,

Who in the void, as we upon
This melancholy sea,
Finds labour and allegiance done,
And Self begin to be.

Louise Imogen Guiney (1861-1920)

PORTRAIT

Her significance lies
in an automatic conscience;
in a mind picked up after every punctual meal
in family virtues sewn on with a hand of steel
and family sins ripped off regardless;
in two accurate reproductions of herself
energetically modelled;
and in one small marionette
who gives her his name
and represents her at the polls.

Jeanne D'Orge

KLEPTOMANIAC

She stole his eyes because they shone,
Stole the good things they looked upon;
They were no brighter than her own.

She stole his mouth—her own was fair—
She stole his words, his songs, his prayer;
His kisses too, since they were there.

She stole the journeys of his heart—
Her own, their very counterpart—
His seas and sails, his course and chart.

She stole his strength so fierce and true,
Perhaps for something brave to do;
Wept at his weakness, stole that too.

But she was caught one early morn!
She stood red-handed and forlorn,
And stole his anger and his scorn.

Upon his knee she laid her head,
Refusing to be comforted;
"Unkind—unkind—" was all she said.

Denied she stole; confessed she did;
Glad of such plunder to be rid—
Clutching the place where it was hid.

As he forgave she snatched his soul;
She did not want it, but she stole.

                                    Leonora Speyer (1872-1956)

Few, save the poor, feel for the poor.

                              Letitia Elizabeth Landon (1802-1838)

MEMORIAL SONNET

By many a saint and many a scholar led,
I devised dreams where death was so assailed
That grief became a source where beauty fed.
My dear, my dear . . . the reasoned dream has failed.
Let nobler hearts, or those who loved you less,
Become with sorrow beautiful and wise;
I only know, upon your nothingness
I stare with cold uncomprehending eyes.
Love cannot glorify the loss of love,
Nor loneliness exalt an empty room,
Nor any gracious solace lift above
The cold ironic shadow of a tomb
Whose simple breadth no fire of faith can span
By any pledge of any God or man.

Marjorie Meeker

RENEWAL

Can this be love men yield to me in return
For what I do? I hold a strange belief
That love is not a tribute, nor a leaf
Of laurel, nor a wage the soul can earn
By any kind of doing. The concern
Of love is need, and love is the spare sheaf
We glean from pain—the fruit of patient grief.
Can this be love men yield to me? Nay. I spurn
Their recompense who could so long refrain
From giving. I myself will grant the gift
And prove what loving is. I'll finer sift
My sorrow, make new songs distilled from pain;
Above this hour of bitterness I'll lift
My spirit up and taste my grief again.

Gladys Cromwell (1885-1919)

MIRROR

There is a mirror in my room
Less like a mirror than a tomb,
There are so many ghosts that pass
Across the surface of the glass.

When in the morning I arise
With circles round my tired eyes,
Seeking the glass to brush my hair
My mother's mother meets me there.

If in the middle of the day
I happen to go by that way,
I see a smile I used to know—
My mother, twenty years ago.

But when I rise by candlelight
To feed my baby in the night,
Then whitely in the glass I see
My dead child's face look up at me.

Aline (Mrs Joyce) Kilmer (1888-1941)

PHILOSOPHERS

Philosophers sit in their sylvan hall
And talk of the duties of man,
Of Chaos and Cosmos, Hegal and Kant,
With the oversoul well in the van,
All of their hobbies they amble away
And a terrible dust they make;
Disciples devout both gaze and adore,
As daily they listen and bake.

Louisa May Alcott (1832-1888)

AUTUMN NIGHT

The moon is as complacent as a frog.
She sits in the sky like a blind white stone,
And does not even see Love
As she caresses his face with her contemptuous light.
She reaches her long white shivering fingers
Into the bowels of men.
Her tender superfluous probing into all that pollutes
Is like the immodesty of the mad.
She is a mad woman holding up her dress
So that her white belly shines.
Haughty,
Impregnable,
Ridiculous,
Silent and white as a debauched queen,
Her ecstacy is that of a cold and sensual child.

She is Death enjoying Life
Lasciviously.

Evelyn Scott (1893-   )

INVENTORY

Four be the things I am wiser to know:
Idleness, sorrow, a friend, and a foe.

Four be the things I'd been better without:
Love, curiosity, freckles, and doubt.

Three be the things I shall never attain:
Envy, content, and sufficient champagne.

Three be the things I shall have till I die:
Laughter and hope and a sock in the eye.

Dorothy Parker (1893-1967)

INDIFFERENT CLAY

No doubt this active will,
So bravely steeped in sun,
This will has vanquished Death
And foiled oblivion.

But this indifferent clay,
This fine experienced hand,
So quiet, and these thoughts
That all unfinished stand,

Feel death as though it were
A shadowy caress;
And win and wear a frail
Archaic wistfulness.

Gladys Cromwell (1885-1919)

SONNET XXIV

Down the black highway where no whisper stirs,
No light leans forth from towers touched with dawn;
One with all uncompanioned wanderers,
I straggle forth by bitter magic drawn.
This conquest into chaos offers more
Than a tight roof with tossing trees above,
Intangible environs to explore—
But you were warm, and breathing, and my love.
Never again shall I ignore a storm
As on those other nights when I have lain
Secure in flesh and mind. I am a form
That haunts unending roadways in the rain,
Or stumbles blindly over desert ground—
Seeking the thing no man has ever found.

Shirley Barker

WISHES

The human heart has hidden treaures,
In secret, in silence sealed;—
The thoughts, the hopes, the dreams, the pleasures,
Whose charms were broken if revealed.

Charlotte Bronte (1816-1855), from "Evening Solace"

TREASURES

Do they miss me at home—do they miss me?
"Twould be an assurance most dear,
To know that this moment some loved one
Were saying, "I wish she were here."

Caroline Atherton Briggs Mason (1823-1890)

SONNET TO EDGAR ALLAN POE

On our lone pathway bloomed no earthly hopes:
Sorrow and death were near us, as we stood
Where the dim forest, from the upland slopes,
Swept darkly to the sea. The enchanted wood
Thrilled, as by some foreboding terror stirred;
And as the waves broke on the lonely shore,
In their low monotone, methought I heard
A solemn voice that sighed, "Ye meet no more."
There, while the level sunbeams seemed to burn
Through the long aisles of red, autumnal gloom,—
Where stately, storied cenotaphs inurn
Sweet human hopes, too fair on Earth to bloom,—
Was the bud reaped, whose petals pure and cold
Sleep on my heart till Heaven the flower unfold.

Sarah Helen Whitman (1803-1878)

HUNGER

In that strange city
    Of being poor
I have lived all my life
    And more;

I have lived out from myself
    And from this place
Over through time,
    Through space.

I know what others suffered
    Before me;
No one who is hungry
    Can be quite free.

This is the only suffering there is
    Or was before,
Or will be, ever—
    Being poor.

To lose a lover
    Does not shake the soul
Like a wet and broken shoe,
    Or an empty bowl,

Like the fear of no roof at night,
    And no hand to aid,
And most of all the fear
    Of being afraid.

Afraid of men because
    I have not that shield,
And the sword, of a round small coin
    To wield.

Soul agony is sad,
   but this is worse,
To be broken by the number
   Of pennies in the purse.

Mary Carolyn Davies

MUSIC

The neighbor sits in his window and plays the flute.
From my bed I can hear him,
And the round notes flutter and tap about the room,
And hit against each other,
Blurring into unexpected chords.
It is very beautiful,
With the little flute-notes all about me,
In the darkness.

In the daytime,
The neighbor eats bread and onions with one hand
And copies music with the other.
He is fat and has a bald head,
So I do not look at him,
But run quickly past his window.
There is always the sky to look at,
Or the water in the well!

But when night comes and he plays his flute,
I think of him as a young man,
With gold seals hanging from his watch,
And a blue coat with silver buttons.
As I lie in my bed
The flute-notes push against my ears and lips,
And I go to sleep dreaming.

Amy Lowell (1874-1925)

SONG OF ELGA

Day in melting purple dying,
Blossoms all around me sighing,
Fragrance from the lilies straying,
Zephyr with my ringlets playing.
Ye but waken my distress:
I am sick of loneliness.
Thou to whom I love to hearken,
Come ere night around me darken:
Though thy softness but deceive me,
Say thou'rt true, and I'll believe thee.
    Veil, if ill, thy soul's intent:
    Let me think it innocent!

Save thy toiling, spare thy treasure:
All I ask is friendship's pleasure:
Let the shining ore lie darkling;
Bring no gem in lustre sparkling;
    Gifts and gold are naught to me:
    I would only look on thee;

Tell to thee the high-wrought feeling,
Ecstacy but in revealing;
Paint to thee the deep sensation,
Rapture in participation,
    Yet but torture, if comprest
    In a lone unfriendly breast.

Absent still? Ah, come and bless me!
Let these eyes again caress thee.
Once, in caution, I could fly thee.
Now I nothing could deny thee.
    In a look if death there be,
    Come, and I will gaze on thee!

Maria Gowen Brooks (1795-1845)

TRUE LOVE

I think true love is never blind,
But brings an added light,
An inner vision quick to find
The beauties hid from common sight.

Phoebe Cary (1824-1874)

LOVE

Love is anterior to life,
Posterior to death,
Initial of creation, and
The exponent of breath.

Emily Dickinson (1830-1886)

JOHNNY APPLESEED

Let all unselfish spirits heed
The story of Johnny Appleseed.
He had another and prouder name
In far New England, whence he came.
By this title and this alone,
Was the kindly wanderer loved and known.

Elizabeth Akers Allen (1832-1911)

I do not own an inch of land,
But all I see is mine.

Lucy Larcom (1824-1893)

DREAM

I slept and dreamed that life was beauty.
I woke—and found that life was duty;
Was my dream, then, a shadowy lie?
Toil on, sad heart, courageously,
And thou shalt find thy dream shall be
A noonday light and truth to thee.

Ellen Sturgis Hooper (1816-1841), from "Beauty and Duty"

YOUR KISS

I believe if I should die
And you should kiss my eyelids when I lie
Cold, dead, and dumb to all the world contains,
The folded orbs would open at thy breath,
And from its exile in the isles of death,
Life would come gladly back along my veins.

Mary Ashley Townsend (1836-1901)

CLEVER PEOPLE

If all the good people were clever,
    And all the clever people were good,
The world would be nicer than ever
    We thought that it possibly could.

But somehow, 'tis seldom or never
    The two hit it off as they should;
The good are so harsh to the clever,
    The clever so rude to the good.

Elizabeth Wordsworth (1840-1932)

LOVE-KNOTS

Tying her bonnet under her chin,
She tied her raven ringlets in;
But not alone in the silken snare
Did she catch her lovely floating hair,
For, tying her bonnet under her chin,
She tied a young man's heart within.

Nora Perry (1832-1896)

TONIGHT

Bend low, O dusky Night,
    And give my spirit rest,
    Hold me to your deep breast,
And put old cares to flight.
Give back the lost delight
    That once my soul possessed,
    When love was loveliest.

Louise Chandler Moulton (1835-1908)

NOT KNOWING

I see not a step before me as I tread on
    another year;
But I've left the past in God's keeping,
    —the Future His mercy shall clear;
And what looks dark in the distance,
    may brighten as I draw near.

Mary Gardiner Brainard (1837-1905)

POWER

The Bluebell is the sweetest flower
That waves in summer air:
Its blossoms have the mightiest power
To soothe my spirit's care.

Emily Bronte (1818-1848), from The "Bluebell"

PEDIGREE

The pedigree of honey
Does not concern the bee;
A clover, any time, to him
Is aristocracy.

Emily Dickinson (1830-1886)

SHADOWS

This learned I from the shadow of a tree,
That to and fro did sway against a wall,
Our shadow selves, our influence, may fall
Where we ourselves can never be.

Anna E. Hamilton (1843-1876)

PAGEANTRY

Strange we never prize the music
Till the sweet-voiced bird has flown,
Strange that we should slight the violets
Till the lovely flowers are gone.

Mary Riley Smith (18742-1927)

BLINDNESS

There cannot be found in the animal kingdom a bat, or any other creature, so blind in its own range of circumstance and connection, as the greater majority of human beings are in the bosoms of their families.

Helen Hunt Jackson (1831-1885)

CROWN

I do not ask for any crown
But that which all may win;
Nor try to conquer any world
Except the one within.

Louisa May Alcott (1832-1888)

FAME

The moment an audacious head is lifted one inch above the general level, pop! goes the unerring rifle of some biographical sharpshooter, and it is all over with the unhappy owner.

Mary Abigail Dodge ("Gail Hamilton") (1833-1896)

Out of the strain of the Doing,
Into the peace of the Done.

Julia Louise Matilda Woodruff (1833-1909)

Better build schoolrooms for "the boy"—
Than cells and gibbets for "the man."

Eliza Cook (1818-1889)

HAPPY LETTER

"Going to him! Happy letter! tell him—
Tell him the page I didn't write;
Tell him I only said the syntax,
And left the verb and pronoun out.

Emily Dickinson (1830-1886)

GRAVES

I lingered round them, under that benign sky: watched
the moths fluttering among the heath and hare-bells; listened
to the soft wind breathing through the grass; and wondered
how any one would ever imagine unquiet slumbers for the
sleepers in that quiet earth.

Emily Bronte (1818-1848), from Wuthering Heights

COMFORT

You needn't be trying to comfort me—
I tell you my dolly is dead!
There's no use in saying she isn't,
With a crack like that in her head.

Margaret Thomson Janvier (1845-1913)

SHEPHERDESS

She walks—the lady of my delight—
A shepherdess of sheep.
Her thoughts are sheep. She keeps them white;
She guards them from the steep.

Alice Meynell (1847-1922)

OLD BUSINESS

Where is the promise of my years,
    Once written on my brow?
Ere errors, agonies, and fears
Brought with them all that speaks in tears,
Ere I had sunk beneath my peers;-
    Where sleeps that promise now?

Ada Isaacs Menken (1835-1868)

SORROW

Silence is no certain token
    That no secret grief is there;
Sorrow which is never spoken
    Is the heaviest load to bear.

Frances Ridley Havergal (1836-1879)

KNOWLEDGE

The common stock of intellectual enjoyment should not be difficult of access because of the economic position of him who would approach it.

Jane Addams (1860-1935)

This is the bitterest of all, to wear the yoke of our wrong-doing.

George Eliot (1819-1880)

POETRY

If I read a book and it makes my whole body so cold no fire can ever warm me, I know that is poetry. If I feel physically as if the top of my head were taken off, I know that is poetry. These are the only ways I know it. Is there any other way?

Emily Dickinson (1830-1886)

COMPANION

Across the narrow beach we flit,
    One little sand piper and I;
And fast I gather, bit by bit,
    The scattered drift wood, bleached and dry.
The wild waves reach their hands for it,
    The wild wind raves, the tide runs high,
As up and down the beach we flit,
    One little sand piper and I.

Celia Laighton Thaxter (1835-1894)

DUTY

Long, long years I've rung the curfew from
    that gloomy, shadowed tower;
Every evening, just at sunset, it has told
    the twilight hour.
I have done my duty ever, tried to do it
    just and right,
Now I'm old I will not falter,—Curfew it
    must ring tonight.

Rose Hartwick Thorpe (1850-1939)

TO GIVE

There are loyal hearts, there are spirits brave,
There are souls that are pure and true;
Then give to the world the best you have,
And the best will come back to you.

Mary Ainge De Vere ("Madeline Bridges") (1844-1920)

HARBORS

A harbor, even if it is a little harbor, is a good thing, since adventurers come into it as well as go out, and the life in it grows strong, because it takes something from the world and has something to give in return.

Sarah Orne Jewett (1849-1909)

ROSES

There is always room for beauty: memory
A myriad lovely blossoms may enclose,
But, whatsoever hath been, there still must be
Room for another rose.

Florence Earle Coates (1850-1927)

DAISIES

Daisies won't tell, dear, come kiss me, do,
Tell me you love me. Say you'll be true.
And I will promise always to be
Tender and faithful, sweetheart, to thee.

Anita Owen

LEGS

It is principally for the sake of the leg that a change in the dress of man is so much to be desired. . . . The leg is the best part of the figure . . . and the best leg is the man's. Man should no longer disguise the long lines, the strong forms, in those lengths of piping or tubing that are of all garments the most stupid.

Alice Meynell (1847-1922)

ART

If you are an artist, may no love of wealth or fame or admiration and no fear of blame or misunderstanding make you ever paint, with pen or brush, an ideal or a picture of external life otherwise than as you see it.

Olive Schreiner ("Ralph Iron") (1855-1920)

AUTUMN

The morns are meeker than they were,
    The nuts are getting brown;
The berry's cheek is plumper,
    The rose is out of town.

The maple wears a gayer scarf,
    The field a scarlet gown.
Lest I should be old fashioned,
    I'll put a trinket on.

Emily Dickinson (1830-1886)

KINDNESS

Hurt no living thing:
  Ladybird, no butterfly,
Nor moth with dusty wing,
  Nor cricket chirping cheerily,
Nor grasshopper so light of leap,
  Nor dancing gnat, nor beetle fat,
Nor harmless worms that creep.

Christina Rossetti (1830-1894)

FRINGED GENTIANS

Near where I live there is a lake
As blue as blue can be; winds make
It dance as they go blowing by.
I think it curtsies to the sky.

It's just a lake of lovely flowers,
And my Mamma says they are ours;
But they are not like those we grow
To be our very own, you know.

We have a splendid garden, there
Are lots of flowers everywhere;
Roses, and pinks, and four-o-clocks,
And hollyhocks, and evening stocks.

Mamma lets us pick them, but never
Must we pick any gentians—ever!
For if we carried them away
They'd die of homesickness that day.

Amy Lowell (1874-1925)

LOVELY THINGS

Stars over snow
   And in the west a planet
Swinging below a star—
   Look for a lovely thing and you will find it,
It is not far—
   It never will be far.

Sarah Teasdale (1884-1933)

MORNING

Will there really be morning?
   Is there such a thing as day?
Could I see it from the mountains
   If I were as tall as they?

Has it feet like water lilies?
   Has it feathers like a bird?
Is it brought from famous countries
   Of which I have never heard?

Oh, some scholar! Oh, some sailor!
   Oh, some wise man from the skies!
Please to tell a little pilgrim
   Where the place called morning lies.

Emily Dickinson (1830-1886)

Life appears to me too short to be spent in nursing animosity or registering wrong.

Charlotte Bronte (1816-1855)

MARY'S LAMB

Mary had a little lamb,
　　Its fleece was white as snow;
And everywhere that Mary went,
　　The lamb was sure to go.

He followed her to school one day,
　　Which was against the rule;
It made the children laugh and play
　　To see the lamb at school.

And so the teacher turned him out,
　　But still he lingered near,
And waited patiently about
　　Till Mary did appear.

Then he ran to her and laid
　　His head upon her arm,
As if he said, "I'm not afraid—
　　You'll keep me from all harm."

"What makes the lamb love Mary so?"
　　The eager children cried.
"Oh, Mary loves the lamb, you know,"
　　The teacher quick replied.

And you each gentle animal
　　In confidence may bind,
And make them follow at your will,
　　If you are only kind.

Sarah Josepha Hale (1790-1879)

We can do anything we want to if we stick to it long enough.

Helen Keller (1880-1968)

HOPE

Children of yesterday,
    Heirs of tomorrow,
What are you weaving?
    Labor and sorrow?
Look to your looms again,
    Faster and faster
Fly the great shuttles
    Prepared by the Master.
Life's in the loom,
Room for it — room!

Mary Artemisia Lathbury (1841-1913)

JOAN

Along the thousand roads of France,
Now there, now here, swift as a glance,
A cloud, a mist blown down the sky,
Good Joan of Arc goes riding by.

In Domremy at candlelight,
The orchards blowing rose and white
About the shadowy houses lie;
And Joan of Arc goes riding by.

On Avignon there falls a hush,
Brief as the singing of a thrush
Across old gardens April-high;
And Joan of Arc goes riding by.

The women bring the apples in,
Round Arles when the long gusts begin,
Then sit them down to sob and cry;
And Joan of Arc goes riding by.

Lizette Woodworth Reese (1856-1935)

SOMEBODY'S MOTHER

The woman was old and ragged and gray
And bent with the chill of the Winter's day.
The street was wet with a recent snow
And the woman's feet were aged and slow.
She stood at the crossing and waited long,
Alone, uncared for, amid the throng
Of human beings who passed her by
Nor heeded the glance of her anxious eye.
Down the street, with laughter and shout,
Glad in the freedom of "school let out,"
Came the boys like a flock of sheep,
Hailing the snow piled white and deep.
Past the woman so old and gray
Hastened the children on their way.
Nor offered a helping hand to her—
So meek, so timid, afraid to stir
Lest the carriage wheels or the horses' feet
Should crowd her down in the slippery street.
At last came one of the merry troop,
The gayest laddie of all the group;
He paused beside her and whispered low,
"I'll help you cross, if you wish to go."
Her aged hand on his strong young arm
She placed, and so, without hurt or harm,
He guided the trembling feet along,
Proud that his own were firm and strong,
Then back again to his friends he went,
His young heart happy and well content.
"She's somebody's mother, boys, you know,
For all she's aged and poor and slow.
"And I hope some fellow will lend a hand
To help my mother, you understand,
"If ever she's poor and old and gray,
When her own dear boy is far away."
And "somebody's mother" bowed low her head

In her home that night, and the prayer she said
Was "God be kind to the noble boy,
Who is somebody's son, and pride and joy!"

Mary Dow Brine

REMEMBRANCE

Cold in the earth—and the deep snow piled
    above thee,
Far, far removed, cold in the dreary grave!
Have I forgot, my only Love, to love thee,
Severed at last by Time's all-severing wave?

Now, when alone, do my thoughts no longer hover
Over the mountains, on that northern shore,
Resting their wings where heath and fern-leaves cover
The noble heart for ever, ever more?

Cold in the earth—and fifteen wild Decembers,
From those brown hills, have melted into spring:
Faithful, indeed, is the spirit that remembers
After such years of change and suffering!

Sweet Love of youth, forgive, if I forget thee,
While the world's tide is bearing me along;
Other desires and other hopes beset me,
Hopes which obscure, but cannot do thee wrong!

No later light has lightened up my heaven,
No second morn has ever shone for me;
All my life's bliss from thy dear life was given,
All my life's bliss is in the grave with thee.

But, when the days of golden dreams had perished,
And even Despair was powerless to destroy;

Then did I learn how existence could be cherished,
Strengthened and fed without the aid of joy.

Then did I check the tears of useless passion—
Weaned my young soul from yearning after thine;
Sternly denied its burning wish to hasten
Down to that tomb already more than mine.

And, even yet, I dare not let it languish,
Dare not indulge in memory's rapturous pain;
Once drinking deep of that divinest anguish,
How could I seek the empty world again?

Emily Bronte (1818-1848)

WHEN I AM DEAD, MY DEAREST

When I am dead, my dearest,
Sing no sad songs for me;
Plant thou no roses at my head,
Nor shady crypress-tree:
Be the green grass above me
With showers and dewdrips wet;
And if thou wilt, remember,
And if thou wilt, forget.

I shall not see the shadows,
I shall not feel the rain;
I shall not hear the nightingale
Sing on, as if in pain:
And dreaming through the twilight
That doth not rise nor set,
Haply I may remember,
And haply may forget.

Christina Rossetti (1830-1894)

BOOKS

He ate and drank the precious words,
His spirit grew robust;
He knew no more that he was poor,
Nor that his frame was dust.
He danced along the dingy days,
And this bequest of wings
Was but a book. What liberty
A loosened spirit brings!

Emily Dickinson (1830-1886)

IN THE GLOAMING

In the gloaming, oh, my darling,
When the lights are dim and low,
And the quiet shadows falling,
Softly come, and softly go;
When the winds are sobbing faintly,
With a gentle, unknown woe;
Will you think of me and love me?
As you did once long ago?

In the gloaming, oh, my darling,
Think not bitterly of me.
Tho' I passed away in silence,
Left you lonely, set you free;
For my heart was crushed with longing,
What had been could never be;
It was best to leave you thus, dear,
Best for you and best for me.
It was best to leave you thus,
Best for you and best for me.

Meta Orred

THE OLD STOIC

Riches I hold in light esteem,
And love I laugh to scorn;
And lust of fame was but a dream
That vanished with the morn:

And if I pray, the only prayer
That moves my lips for me
Is, "Leave the heart that now I bear,
And give me liberty!"

Yes, as my swift days near their goal,
'Tis all that I implore—
Through life and death a chainless soul,
With courage to endure.

Emily Bronte (1818-1848)

I SHALL NOT CARE

When I am dead and over me bright April
    Shakes out her rain-drenched hair,
Though you should lean above me broken-hearted,
    I shall not care.

I shall have peace, as leafy trees are peaceful
    When rain bends down the bough;
And I shall be more silent and cold-hearted
    Than you are now.

Sarah Teasdale (1884-1933)

WHERE THERE'S A WILL THERE'S A WAY

We have faith in old proverbs full surely,
    For Wisdom has traced what they tell,
And Truth may be drawn up as purely
    From them, as it may from "a well."
Let us question the thinkers and doers,
    And hear what they honestly say;
And you'll find they believe, like bold wooers,
    In "Where there's a will there's a way."

The hills have been high for man's mounting,
    The woods have been dense for his axe,
The stars have been thick for his counting,
    The sands have been wide for his tracks,
The sea has been deep for his diving,
    The poles have been broad for his sway,
But bravely he's proved in his striving,
    That "Where there's a will there's a way."

Have ye vices that ask a destroyer?
    Or passions that need your control?
Let Reason become your employer,
    And your body be ruled by your soul.

Fight on, though ye bleed in the trial,
    Resist with all strength that ye may;
Ye may conquer Sin's host by denial;
    For "Where there's a will there's a way."

Have ye Poverty's pinching to cope with?
    Does Suffering weigh down your might?
Only call up a spirit to hope with,
    And dawn may come out of the night.
Oh! much may be done by defying
    The ghosts of Despair and Dismay,

And much may be gained by relying
  On "Where there's a will there's a way."

Should ye see, afar off, that worth winning,
  Set out on the journey with trust
And ne'er heed if your path at beginning
  Should be among brambles and dust.
Though it is but by footsteps ye do it
  And hardships may hinder and stay;
Walk with faith, and be sure you'll get through it;
  For "Where there's a will there's a way."

Eliza Cook (1818-1889)

IF THOU MUST LOVE ME

If thou must love me, let it be for naught
Except for love's sake only. Do not say,
"I love her for her smile—her look—her way
Of speaking gently,—for a trick of thought
That falls in well with mine, and certes brought
A sense of pleasant ease on such a day"—
For these things in themselves, Beloved, may
Be changed, or change for thee—and love, so wrought,
May be unwrought so. Neither love me for
Thine own dear pity's wiping my cheeks dry:
A creature might forget to weep, who bore
Thy comfort long, and lose thy love thereby!
But love me for love's sake, that evermore
Thou mayst love on, through love's eternity.

Elizabeth Barrett Browning (1806-1861)

A woman can stand anything but being forgotten, not being needed.

Mary Stewart Cutting

KEEP A STIFF UPPER LIP

There has something gone wrong,
    My brave boy, it appears,
For I see your proud struggle
    To keep back the tears.
That is right; when you cannot
    Give trouble the slip,
Then bear it, still keeping
    A stiff upper lip!

Though you cannot escape
    Disappointment and care,
There's one thing you can do, —
    It is, learn how to bear.
If when for life's prizes
    You're running, you trip,
Get up, start again,
    Keep a stiff upper lip!

Let your hands and your conscience
    Be honest and clean;
Scorn to touch or to think
    Of the thing that is mean;
But hold on to the pure
    And the right with firm grip;
And though hard be the task,
    Keep a stiff upper lip!

Through childhood, through manhood,
    Through life to the end,
Struggle bravely and stand
    By your colors, my friend;
Only yield when you must,
    Never give up the ship,
But fight on to the last
    With a stiff upper lip.

Phoebe Cary (1824-1871)

EUCLID ALONE

Euclid alone has looked on Beauty bare.
Let all who prate of Beauty hold their peace,
And lay them prone upon the earth and cease
To ponder on themselves, the while they stare
At nothing, intricately drawn nowhere
In shapes of shifting lineage; let geese
Gabble and hiss, but heroes seek release
From dusty bondage into luminous air.
O blinding hour, O holy, terrible day,
When first the shaft into his vision shone
Of light anatomized! Euclid alone
Has looked on Beauty bare. Fortunate they
Who, though once only and then but far away,
Have heard her massive sandal set on stone.

Edna St. Vincent Millay (1892-1950)

TALENT

The unused talent now going to waste among persons who think they are on the shelf could win world peace, mitigate racial tensions, help economically less advanced people . . . and give new hope to life throughout the world.

Joy Elmer Morgan

I had a pleasant time with my mind, for it was happy.

Louisa May Alcott (1832-1888)

Whatever comes, this too shall pass away.

Ella Wheeler Wilcox (1855-1919)

PADDLE YOUR OWN CANOE

Voyager upon life's sea,
    To yourself be true;
And where'er your lot may be,
    Paddle your own canoe.
Never, though the winds may rave,
    Falter nor look back,
But upon the darkest wave
    Leave a shining track.

Nobly dare the wildest storm,
    Stem the hardest gale,
Brave of heart and strong of arm,
    You will never fail.
When the world is cold and dark,
    Keep an end in view,
And toward the beacon mark
    Paddle your own canoe.

Every wave that bears you on
    To the silent shore,
From its sunny source has gone
    To return no more:
Then let not an hour's delay
    Cheat you of your due;
But while it is called to-day,
    Paddle your own canoe.

If your birth denied you wealth,
    Lofty state, and power,
Honest fame and hardy health
    Are a better dower;
But if these will not suffice,
    Golden gain pursue,
And to win the glittering prize,
    Paddle your own canoe.

Would you wrest the wreath of fame
  From the hand of Fate?
Would you write a deathless name
  With the good and great?
Would you bless your fellowmen?
  Heart and soul imbue
With the holy task, and then
  Paddle your own canoe.

Would you crush the tyrant Wrong,
  In the world's fierce fight?
With a spirit brave and strong,
  Battle for the Right;
And to break the chains that bind
  The many to the few—
To enfranchise slavish mind,
  Paddle your own canoe.

Nothing great is lightly won,
  Nothing won is lost—
Every good deed nobly done,
  Will repay the cost;
Leave to Heaven, in humble trust,
  All you will to do;
But if you succeed, you must
  Paddle your own canoe.

Sarah K. Bolton

CHRISTMAS

We ring the bells and we raise the strain,
We hang up garlands everywhere,
And bid the tapers twinkle fair,
And feast and frolic—and then we go
Back to the same old lives again.

Susan Coolidge (1835-1905)

CASABIANCA

In the battle of the Nile, thirteen-year-old Casabianaca, son of the Admiral of the Orient, remained at his post after the ship had taken fire and the guns had been abandoned. He perished with the ship.

The boy stood on the burning deck,
Whence all but he had fled;
The flame that lit the battle's wreck,
Shone round him o'er the dead.

Yet beautiful and bright he stood,,
As born to rule the storm;
A creature of heroic blood,
A proud though childlike form.

The flames rolled on; he would not go
Without his father's word;
That father, faint in death below,
His voice no longer heard.

He called aloud, "Say, Father, say,
If yet my task is done!"
He knew not that the chieftain lay
Unconscious of his son.

"Speak, Father!" once again he cried,
"If I may yet be gone!"
—And but the blooming shots replied,
And fast the flames rolled on.

Upon his brow he felt their breath,
And in his waving hair;
And looked from that lone post of death
In still yet brave despair;

And shouted but once more aloud,
"My Father! Must I stay?"

While o'er him fast, through sail and shroud,
The wreathing fires made way.

They wrapt the ship in splendor wild,
They caught the flag on high,
And streamed above the gallant child,
Like banners in the sky.

There came a burst of thunder sound;
The boy—Oh! Where was *he?*
—Ask of the winds, that far around
With fragments strewed the sea;—

With shroud, and mast, and pennon fair,
That well had borne their part,—
But the noblest thing that perished there
Was that young, faithful heart.

Felicia Dorothea Hemans (1793-1835)

OPPORTUNITY

Learn to make the most of life,
Lose no happy day,
Time will never bring thee back
Chances swept away!

Leave no tender word unsaid,
Love while love shall last;
"The mill cannot grind
With the water that is past."

Sarah Doudney (1843-1926)

RECUERDO

We were very tired, we were very merry—
We had gone back and forth all night on the ferry.
It was bare and bright, and smelled like a stable—
But we looked into a fire, we leaned across a table,
We lay on a hill-top underneath the moon;
And the whistles kept blowing, and the dawn came soon.

We were very tired, we were very merry—
We had gone back and forth all night on the ferry;
And you ate an apple, and I ate a pear,
From a dozen of each we had bought somewhere;
And the sky went wan, and the wind came cold,
And the sun rose dripping, a bucketful of gold.

We were very tired, we were very merry,
We had gone back and forth all night on the ferry.
We hailed, "Good morrow, mother!" to a shawl-covered
head,
And bought a morning paper, which neither of us read;
And she wept, "God bless you!" for the apples and pears,
And we gave her all our money but our subway fares.

                                    Edna St. Vincent Millay (1892-1950)

THE TOYS

My little Son, who looked from thoughtful eyes
And moved and spoke in quiet grown-up wise,
Having my law the seventh time disobeyed,
I struck him, and dismissed
With hard words and unkissed,
—His Mother, who was patient, being dead.
Then, fearing lest his grief should hinder sleep,

I visited his bed,
But found him slumbering deep,

With darkened eyelids, and their lashes yet
From his late sobbing wet.
And I, with moan,
Kissing away his tears, left others of my own;
For, on a table drawn beside his head,
He had put, within his reach,
A box of counters and a red-veined stone,
A piece of glass abraded by the beach,
And six or seven shells,
A bottle with bluebells,

And two French copper coins, ranged there with
    careful art,
To comfort his sad heart.
So when that night I prayed
To God, I wept, and said:
Ah, when at last we lie with tranced breath,
Not vexing Thee in death,
And Thou rememberest of what toys
We made our joys,

How weakly understood
Thy great commanded good,
Then, fatherly not less
Thank I whom Thou hast moulded from the clay,
Thou'lt leave Thy wrath, and say,
"I will be sorry for their childishness."

Coventry Patmore (1823-1896)

STILL PULLING

When I see a Weed I
    have to pull it.

Florence Foy (1898-   )

SLEEP

Of all the thoughts of God that are
Borne inward unto souls afar,
Among the Psalmist's music deep,
Now tell me if that any is
For gift or grace surpassing this,—
"He giveth his beloved sleep"?

What would we give to our beloved?
The hero's heart, to be unmoved,—
The poet's star-tuned harp, to sweep,—
The patriot's voice, to teach and rouse,—
The monarch's crown, to light the brows?
"He giveth his beloved sleep."

What do we give to our beloved?
A little faith, all undisproved,—
A little dust, to overweep,—
And bitter memories, to make
The whole earth blasted for our sake,
"He giveth his beloved sleep."

"Sleep soft, beloved!" we sometimes say,
But have no tune to charm away
Sad dreams that through the eyelids creep;
But never doleful dream again
Shall break the happy slumber when
"He giveth his beloved sleep."

O earth, so full of dreary noise!
O men, with wailing in your voice!
O delved gold the wailers heap!
O strife, O curse, that o'er it fall!
God strikes a silence through you all,
And "giveth his beloved sleep."

His dews drop mutely on the hill,
His cloud above it saileth still,
Though on its slope men sow and reap;
More softly than the dew is shed,
Or cloud is floated overhead,
"He giveth his beloved sleep."

For me, my heart, that erst did go
Most like a tired child at a show,
That sees through tears the mummers leap,
Would now its wearied vision close,
Would childlike on His love repose
Who "giveth his beloved sleep."

Elizabeth Barrett Browning (1806-1861)

A SONNET ON A MONKEY

O lovely O most charming pug
Thy graceful air and heavenly mug
The beauties of his mind do shine
And every bit is shaped so fine
Your very tail is most divine
Your teeth is whiter than the snow
You are a great buck and a bow
Your eyes are of so fine a shape
More like a christian's than an ape
His cheeks is like the rose's blume
Your hair is like the raven's plume
His nose's cast is of the roman
He is a very pretty woman
I could not get a rhyme for roman
And was obliged to call him woman.

Marjory Fleming, Age 8

SOLITUDE

Laugh, and the world laughs with you;
    Weep, and you weep alone,
For the sad old earth must borrow its mirth,
    But has trouble enough of its own.
Sing, and the hills will answer;
    Sigh, it is lost on the air,
The echoes bound to a joyful sound,
    But shrink from voicing care.

Rejoice, and men will seek you;
    Grieve, and they turn and go.
They want full measure of all your pleasure,
    But they do not need your woe.
Be glad, and your friends are many;
    Be sad, and you lose them all,—
There are none to decline your nectared wine,
    But alone you must drink life's gall.

Feast, and your halls are crowded;
    Fast, and the world goes by.
Succeed and give, and it helps you live,
    But no man can help you die.
There is room in the halls of pleasure
    For a long and lordly train,
But one by one we must all file on
    Through the narrow aisles of pain.

Ella Wheeler Wilcox (1855-1919)

CREDIT

You can take no credit for beauty at sixteen. But if you
are beautiful at sixty, it will be your own soul's doing.

Marie Carmichael Stopes (1880-1958)

ROCK ME TO SLEEP

Backward, turn backward, O Time, in your flight,
Make me a child again just for to-night!
Mother, come back from the echoless shore,
Take me again to your heart as of yore;
Kiss from my forehead the furrows of care,
Smooth the few silver threads out of my hair;
Over my slumbers your loving watch keep;—
Rock me to sleep, Mother—rock me to skeep!

Bakcward, flow backward, O tide of the years!
I am so weary of toil and of tears—
Toil without recompense, tears all in vain—
Take them, and give me my childhood again!
I have grown weary of dust and decay—
Weary of flinging my soul-wealth away;
Weary of sowing for others to reap;—
Rock me to sleep, Mother—rock me to sleep!

Tired of the hollow, the base, the untrue,
Mother, O Mother, my heart calls for you!
Many a summer the grass has grown green,
Blossomed and faded, our faces between:
Yet, with strong yearning and passionate pain,
Long I to-night for your presence again.
Come from the silence so long and so deep;—
Rock me to sleep, Mother—rock me to sleep!

Over my heart, in the days that are flown,
No love like mother-love ever has shone;
No other worship abides and endures—
Faithful, unselfish, and patient like yours:
None like a mother can charm away pain
From the sick soul and the world-weary brain.
Slumber's soft calms o'er my heavy lids creep;—
Rock me to sleep, Mother—rock me to sleep!

Come, let your brown hair, just lighted with gold,
Fall on your shoulders again as of old;
Let it drop over my forehead to-night,
Shading my faint eyes away from the light;
For with its sunny-edged shadows once more
Haply will throng the sweet visions of yore;
Lovingly, softly, its bright billows sweep;—
Rock me to sleep, Mother—rock me to sleep!

Mother, dear Mother, the years have been long
Since I last listened your lullaby song;
Sing, then, and unto my soul it shall seem
Womanhood's years have been only a dream.
Clasped to your heart in a loving embrace,
With your light lashes just sweeping my face,
Never hereafter to wake or to weep;—
Rock me to sleep, Mother—rock me to sleep!

Elizabeth Akers Allen (1832-1911)

BOLDNESS

I could not at any age be content to take my place in a corner by the fireside and simply look on. Life was meant to be lived. One must never, for whatever reason, turn one's back on life.

Eleanor Roosevelt (1884-1962)

SCARS

There are words the point of which sting the heart through the course of a whole life.

Frederika Bremer (1801-1865)

FRIENDSHIP

Oh, the comfort, the inexpressible comfort, of feeling safe with a person, having neither to weigh thoughts, nor measure words—but pouring them all right out—just as they are—chaff and grain together—certain that a faithful hand will take and sift them—keep what is worth keeping—and with the breath of kindness blow the rest away.

Dinah Maria Mulock Craik (1826-1887)

SONG

I can't be talkin' of love, dear,
I can't be talkin' of love.
If there be one thing I can't talk of
That one thing do be love.

But that's not sayin' that I'm not lovin'—
Still water, you know, runs deep,
An' I do be lovin' so deep, dear,
I be lovin' you in my sleep.

But I can't be talkin' of love, dear,
I can't be talkin' of love,
If there be one thing I can't talk of
That one thing do be love.

Esther Mathews

WAITING

To find the loved ones waiting on the shore,
More beautiful, more precious than before.

Ella Wheeler Wilcox (1855-1919)

YOUTH AND BEAUTY

I think we are inclined to forget that youth and beauty are [after] all . . . only lures. They are not binders . . . We stress too much the externals and forget too much the realities . . . There are greater hazards to marriage than attraction for other people.

                                                            Margaret W. Jackson

START NOW

It will take,
I think,
A long time
To learn how.

Should we not
Start now?

                                                            Carol Lynn Pearson

A SUMMER MORNING

I saw dawn creep across the sky,
And all the gulls go flying by.
I saw the sea put on its dress
Of blue mid-summer loveliness,
And heard the trees begin to stir
Green arms of pine and juniper.
I heard the wind call out and say:
"Get up, my dear, it is to-day!"

                                        Rachel Field (1894-1942), *The Pointed People*

PEACE

There is no peace on earth today
Save the peace in the heart at home with God . . .
No man can be at peace with his neighbor who is not
at peace with himself.

Edna St. Vincent Millay (1892-1950)

ONE LIFE

Only one life to live! We all want to do our best with it.
We all want to make the most of it. What is worth while? . . .
The question of life is not, How much time have we? — for in
each day each of us has exactly the same amount: we have
'all there is.' The question is, What shall we do with it? . . .
Time spent in being interrupted is not time lost. . . . There is
time enough given us to do all that God means us to do each
day and to do it gloriously! How do we know but that the in-
terruption we snarl at is the most blessed thing that has come
to us in long days?

Anna R. Lindsay

LESSON

My father taught me that a bill is like a crying baby and
has to be attended to at once.

Anne Morrow Lindbergh (1907-   )

ADVICE

Blessed is the man who, having nothing to say, abstains
from giving us wordy evidence of the fact.

George Eliot (1819-1880)

A FRIEND

Who borrows all your ready cash,
And with it cuts a mighty dash
Proving the lender weak and rash?—
    Your friend!

Who finds out every secret fault,
Misjudges every word and thought,
And makes you pass for worse than nought?—
    Your friend!

Who wins your money at deep play,
Then tells you that the world doth say,
" 'Twere wise from clubs you kept away?"—
    Your friend!

Who sells you, for the longest price,
Horses, a dealer, in a trice,
Would find unsound and full of vice?—
    Your friend!

Who eats your dinner, then looks shrewd;
Wishes you had a cook like Ude,
For then much oftener would intrude?—
    Your friend!

Who tells you that you've shocking wine,
And owns that, though he sports not fine,
Crockford's the only place to dine?—
    Your friend!

Who wheedles you with words most fond
To sign for him a heavy bond,
"Or else, by jove, must quick abscond?"—
    Your friend!

Who makes you all the interest pay,
With principal, some future day,
And laughs at what you then may say?—
    Your friend!

Who makes deep love unto your wife,
Knowing you prize her more than life,
And breeds between you hate and strife?—
    Your friend!

Who, when you've got into a brawl,
Insists that out your man you call,
Then gets you shot, which ends it all?—
    Your friend!!!

Marguerite Power, Countess of Blessington (1789-1849)

LIFE

Life! I know not what thou art,
But know that thou and I must part;
And when, or how, or where we met,
I own to me's a secret yet.
But this I know, when thou art fled,
Where'er they lay these limbs, this head,
No clouds so valueless shall be
As all that then remains of me.

Life! we've been long together,
Through pleasant and through cloudy weather;
    'Tis hard to part when friends are dear;
    Perhaps 'twill cost a sigh, a tear;—
    Then steal away, give little warning,
        Choose thine own time;
Say not Good-night, but in some brighter clime
        Bid me Good-morning!

Anna Letitia Barbauld (1743-1825)

A LOST CHORD

Seated one day at the Organ,
I was weary and ill at ease,
And my fingers wandered idly
Over the noisy keys.

I do not know what I was playing,
Or what I was dreaming then;
But I struck one chord of music,
Like the sound of a great Amen.

It flooded the crimson twilight
Like the close of an angel's Psalm,
And it lay on my fevered spirit
With a touch of infinite calm.

It quieted pain and sorrow,
Like love overcoming strife;
It seemed the harmonious echo
From our discordant life.

It linked all perplexed meanings
Into one perfect peace,
And trembled away into silence,
As if it were loath to cease.

I have sought, but I seek it vainly,
That one lost chord divine,
That came from the soul of the Organ
And entered into mine.

It may be that Death's bright angel
Will speak in that chord again, —
It may be that only in Heaven
I shall hear that grand Amen.

Adelaide Procter (1825-1864)

DEEDS

Our deeds still travel with us from afar,
And what we have been makes us what we are.

George Eliot (1819-1880)

CARING

No civilization is complete which does not include the dumb and defenseless of God's creatures within the sphere of charity and mercy.

Queen Victoria (1819-1901)

HAUNTED

For I am haunted night and day
By all the deeds I have not done.
O unattempted loveliness!
O costly valor never won!

Marguerite Wilkinson

ATOMIC COURTESY

To smash the simple atom
All mankind was intent.
Now any day
The atom may
Return the compliment.

Ethel Jacobson

CONVERSATION

The real art of conversation is not only to say the right thing at the right place but to leave unsaid the wrong thing at the tempting moment.

Dorothy Nevill

REMINDERS

My husband never forgets an anniversary—because I won't let him.

Sara M. Tanner

CARES

The little cares that fretted me,
  I lost them yesterday
Among the fields above the sea,
  Among the winds at play;
Among the lowing of the herds,
  The rustling of the trees,
Among the singing of the birds,
  The humming of the bees.

The foolish fears of what may happen
  I cast them all away
Among the clover-scented grass,
  Among the new-mown hay;
Among the husking of the corn
  Where drowsy poppies nod,
Where ill thoughts die and good are born,
  Out in the fields with God.

Elizabeth Barrett Browning (1806-1861)

AMERICAN PASTIME

Take me out to the ballgame,
Let me cheer with the crowd;
Buy me some peanuts and Cracker Jacks
I don't care if I never get back.
So it's root, root, root for the home team;
If they don't win it's a shame.
Then it's one, two, three strikes you're out!
At the old ball game.

Nellie Kelly

COURAGE

The world stand out on either side
No wider than the heart is wide;
Above the world is stretched the sky,—
No higher than the soul is high.
The heart can push the sea and land
Farther away on either hand;
The soul can split the sky in two,
And let the face of God shine through.
But East and West will pinch the heart
That can not keep them pushed apart;
And he whose soul is flat—the sky
Will cave in on him by and by.

Edna St. Vincent Millay (1892-1950), from "Renascence"

TRIFLES

A life devoted to trifles, not only takes away the inclination, but the capacity for higher pursuits.

Hannah More (1745-1833)

INNER VOICE

The voice of conscience is so delicate that it is easy to stifle it; but it is also so clear that it is impossible to mistake it.

Madame de Stael (1766-1817)

DEATH

We understand death for the first time when he puts his hand upon one whom we love.

Madame de Stael (1766-1817)

ALREADY

One of the soundest rules I try to remember when making forecasts in the field of economics . . . is that whatever is to happen is happening already.

Sylvia Porter

GOLF LINKS

The golf links lie so near the mill
That almost every day
The laboring children can look out
And see the men at play.

Sarah N. Cleghorn (1876-1959)

4

INSPIRATIONAL AND REVERENCE

THY GOD, MY GOD?

Intreat me not to leave thee,
Or to return from following after thee:
For whither thou goest,
I will go;
And where thou lodgest,
I will lodge.
Thy people shall be my people,
And thy God my God.
Where thou diest, will I die,
And there will I be buried.
The Lord do so to me, and more also,
If ought but death part thee and me.

Ruth 1:16-17

OUR MOUNTAIN HOME SO DEAR

Our mountain home so dear,
Where crystal waters clear
Flow ever free,
Flow ever free,
While through the valleys wide
The flow'rs on every side,
Blooming in stately pride,
Are fair to see.

We'll roam the verdant hills,
And by the sparkling rills
Pluck the wild flow'rs,
Pluck the wild flow'rs,
The fragrance on the air,
The landscape bright and fair,
And sunshine every-where
Make pleasant hours.

In sylvan depth and shade,
In forest and in glade,
Wher-e're we pass,
Wher-e'er we pass,
The hand of God we see,
In leaf and bud and tree,
Or bird or humming bee,
Or blade of grass.

The stream-let, flow'r, and sod
Be-speak the words of God;
And all combine,
And all combine,
With most transporting grace,
His handiwork to trace,
Thru nature's smiling face,
In art divine.

Emmeline B. Wells (1828-1921)

LAST LINES

No coward soul is mine,
No trembler in the world's storm-troubled sphere:
   I see Heaven's glories shine,
And faith shines equal, arming me from fear.

   O God within my breast,
Almighty, ever-present Deity!
   Life—that in me hath rest,
As I, undying Life, have power in thee!

   Vain are the thousand creeds
That move men's hearts, unalterably vain;
   Worthless as withered weeds,
Or idlest froth amid the boundless main,

   To waken doubt in one
Holding so fast by thine infinity;
   So surely anchored on
The steadfast rock of immortality.

   With wide-embracing love
Thy spirit animates eternal years,
   Pervades and broods above,
Changes, sustains, dissolves, creates, and rears.

   Though earth and moon were gone,
And suns and universes ceased to be,
   And Thou wert left alone,
Every existence would exist in Thee.

   There is not room for Death,
Nor atom that his might could render void:
   Thou—Thou art Being and Breath,
And what Thou art may never be destroyed.

                   Emily Bronte (1818-1848)

I HAVE WORK ENOUGH TO DO

I have work enough to do,
    Ere the sun goes down,
For myself and kindred too,
    Ere the sun goes down:
Ev'ry idle whisper stilling
    With a purpose firm and willing,
All my daily tasks fulfilling,
    Ere the sun goes down.

I must speak the loving word,
    Ere the sun goes down.
I must let my voice be heard,
    Ere the sun goes down:
Ev'ry cry of pity heeding,
    For the injured interceding,
To the light the lost ones leading,
    Ere the sun goes down.

As I journey on my way,
    Ere the sun goes down,
God's commands I must obey,
    Ere the sun goes down.
There are sins that need confessing;
    There are wrongs that need redressing
If I would obtain the blessing,
    Ere the sun goes down.

Josephine Pollard (1834-1892)

LILIES

I thought I saw white clouds, but no!—
    Bending across the fence,
    White lilies in a row!

Shiko, from *Little Pictures of Japan*

YOU CAN MAKE THE PATHWAY BRIGHT

You can make the pathway bright,
  Fill the soul with heaven's light,
If there's sunshine in your heart;
  Turning darkness into day,
As the shadows fly away,
  If there's sunshine in your heart today.

You can speak the gentle word
  To the heart with anger stirred,
If there's sunshine in your heart;
  Tho it seems a little thing,
It will heaven's blessings bring,
  If there's sunshine in your heart today.

You can do a kindly deed
  To your neighbor in his need,
If there's sunshine in your heart;
  And his burden you will share
As you lift his load of care,
  If there's sunshine in your soul today.

You can live a happy life
  In this world of toil and strife,
If there's sunshine in your heart;
  And your soul will glow with love
From the perfect Light above,
  If there's sunshine in your soul today.

Refrain:

If there's sunshine in your heart,
You can send a shining ray
That will turn the night to day;
And your cares will all depart,
If there's sunshine in your heart today.

Helen Silcott Dungan (ca. 1899)

BEHOLD THE GREAT REDEEMER DIE

Behold the great Redeemer die,
   A broken law to satisfy.
He dies a sacrifice for sin,
   He dies a sacrifice for sin,
That man may live and glory win.

While guilty men his pains deride,
   They pierce his hands and feet and side;
And with insulting scoffs and scorns,
   And with insulting scoffs and scorns,
They crown his head with plaited thorns.

Although in agony he hung,
   No murm'ring word escaped his tongue.
His high commission to fulfill,
   His high commission to fulfill,
He magnified his Father's will.

"Father, from me remove this cup.
   Yet, if thou wilt, I'll drink it up.
I've done the work thou gavest me,
   I've done the work thou gavest me;
Receive my spirit unto thee."

He died and at the awful sight
   The sun in shame withdrew its light!
Earth trembled, and all nature sighed
   In dread response, "A God has died!"

He lives—he lives. We humbly now
   Around these sacred symbols bow,
And seek, as Saints of latter days,
   To do his will and live his praise.

Eliza R. Snow (1804-1887)

I'LL GO WHERE YOU WANT ME TO GO

It may not be on the mountain height
　　Or over the stormy sea,
It may not be at the battle's front
　　My Lord will have need of me.
But if, by a still, small voice he calls
　　To paths that I do not know,
I'll answer, dear Lord, with my hand in thine:
　　I'll go where you want me to.

Perhaps today there are loving words
　　Which Jesus would have me speak;
There may be now in the paths of sin
　　Some wand'rer whom I should seek.
O Savior, if thou wilt be my guide,
　　Tho dark and rugged the way,
My voice shall echo the message sweet:
　　I'll say what you want me to say.

There's surely some-where a lowly place
　　In earth's harvest fields so wide
Where I may labor through life's short day
　　For Jesus, the crucified.
So trusting my all to thy tender care,
　　And knowing thou lovest me,
I'll do thy will with a heart sincere;
　　I'll be what you want me to be.

Refrain:

I'll go where you want me to go, dear Lord,
Over mountain or plain or sea;
I'll say what you want me to say, dear Lord;
I'll be what you want me to be.

Mary Brown (1856-1918)

THERE IS SUNSHINE IN MY SOUL TODAY

There is sun-shine in my soul today,
   More glorious and bright
Than glows in any earthly sky,
   For Jesus is my light.

There is music in my soul today,
   A carol to my King,
And Jesus listening can hear
   The songs I cannot sing.

There is spring-time in my soul today,
   For when the Lord is near,
The dove of peace sings in my heart,
   The flow'rs of grace appear.

There is gladness in my soul today,
   And hope and praise and love,
For blessings which he gives me now,
   For joys "laid up" above.

Refrain:

Oh, there's sun-shine, blessed sun-shine
When the peaceful happy moments roll.
When Jesus shows his smiling face,
There's sun-shine in the soul.

Eliza E. Hewitt (1851-1920)

COURAGE

I have observed all day your patience with baby, your obedience and kindness to all. Go on trying, my child. God will give you strength and courage. I shall say a little prayer over you in your sleep. Mother.

Mother of Louisa May Alcott

SWEET IS THE PEACE THE GOSPEL BRINGS

Sweet is the peace the gospel brings
    To seeking minds and true.
With light refulgent on its wings
    It clears the human view.

Its laws and precepts are divine
    And show a Father's care.
Transcendent love and mercy shine
    In each injunction there.

Faithless tradition flees its pow'r,
    And unbelief gives way.
The gloomy clouds, which used to low'r
    Submit to reason's sway.

May we who know the sacred Name
    From every sin depart.
Then will the spirit's constant flame
    Preserve us pure in heart.

Ere long the tempter's power will cease,
    And sin no more annoy,
No wrangling sects disturb our peace,
    Or mar our heartfelt joy.

That which we have in part received
    Will be in part no more,
For he in whom we all believe
    To us will all restore.

In patience, then, let us possess
    Our souls till he appear.
On to our mark of calling press;
    Redemption draweth near.

Mary Ann Morton (1826-1897)

"ROCKED IN THE CRADLE OF THE DEEP"

Rocked in the cradle of the deep
I lay me down in peace to sleep;
Secure I rest upon the wave,
For Thou, O Lord! hast power to save.
I know Thou wilt not slight my call,
For Thou dost mark the sparrow's fall;
And calm and peaceful shall I sleep,
Rocked in the cradle of the deep.

When in the dead of night I lie
And gaze upon the trackless sky,
The star-bespangled heavenly scroll,
The boundless waters as they roll,—
I feel Thy wondrous power to save
From perils of the stormy wave:
Rocked in the cradle of the deep,
I calmly rest and soundly sleep.

And such the trust that still were mine,
Though stormy winds swept o'er the brine,
Or though the tempest's fiery breath
Roused me from sleep to wreck and death.
In ocean cave, still safe with Thee
The germ of immortality!
And calm and peaceful shall I sleep,
Rocked in the cradle of the deep.

Emma Hart Willard (1787-1870)

THE CONVENT

Her hopes, her fears, her joys were all
Bounded within the cloister wall.

CALLED TO SERVE

Called to serve Him, heavenly King of Glory,
Chosen e'er to witness for his name,
Far and wide we tell the Father's story,
Far and wide his love proclaim.

Called to know the richness of his blessing—
Sons and daughters, children of a King—
Glad of heart, his holy name confessing,
Praises unto him we bring.

Refrain:

Onward, ever onward,
As we glory in his name;
Onward, ever onward,
As we glory in his name;
Forward, pressing forward,
As a triumph song we sing.
God our strength will be;
Press forward ever,
Called to serve our King.

Grace Gordon

PRAYERS

If radio's slim fingers can pluck a melody
From night — and toss it over a continent or sea;
If the petalled white notes of a violin
Are blown across the mountains or the city's din;
If songs, like crimson roses, are culled from thin blue air—
Why should mortals wonder if God hears prayer?

Ethel Romig Fuller

STILL FALLS THE RAIN

Still falls the Rain—
Dark as the world of man, black as our loss—
Blind as the nineteen hundred and forty nails upon the
    Cross

Still falls the Rain
With a sound like the pulse of the heart that is changed
    to the hammer beat
In the Potter's Field, and the sound of the impious feet

On the Tomb:
            Still falls the Rain
In the Field of Blood where the small hopes breed and the
    hguman brain
Nurtures its greed, that worm with the brow of Cain.

Still falls the Rain
At the feet of the Starved Man hung upon the Cross,
Christ that each day, each night, nails there, have mercy
    on us—
On Dives and on Lazarus:
Under the Rain the sore and the gold are as one.

Still falls the Rain—
Still falls the Blood from the Starved Man's wounded Side:
He bears in His Heart all wounds,—those of the light
    that died,
The last faint spark
In the self-murdered heart, the woulds of the sad uncompre-
    hending dark,
The woulds of the baited bear,—
The blind and weeping bear whom the keepers beat
On his helpless flesh . . . the tears of the hunted hare.

Still falls the Rain—
Then—"O Ile leape up to my God! who pulles me doune?—
See, see where Christ's blood streames in the firmament."
It flows from the Brow we nailed upon the tree
Deep to the dying, to the thristing heart
That holds the fires of the world,—dark-smirched with pain
As Caesar's laurel crown.

Then sounds the voice of One who, like the heart of man,
Was once a child who among beasts has lain—
"Still do I love, still shed my innocent light, by Blood, for
    thee."

Edith Sitwell (1887-1964)

SELF-ANALYSIS

The tumult of my fretted mind
Gives me expression of a kind;
But it is faulty, harsh, not plain—
My work has the incompetence of pain.

I am consumed with a slow fire,
For righteousness is my desire;
Towards that good goal I cannot whip my will,
I am a tired horse that jibs upon a hill.

I desire Virtue, though I love her not—
I have no faith in her when she is got:
I feat that she will bind and make me slave
And send me songless to the sullen grave.

I am like a man who fears to take a wife,
And frets his soul with wantons all his life.
With rich, unholy foods I stuff my maw;
When I am sick, then I believe in law.

Anna Wickham (1884-   )

THY SOUL IS FREE

'Twas something like the burst from death to life;
From the grave's cerements to the robes of Heaven,
From sin's dominion, and from passion's strife,
To the pure freedom of a soul forgiven;
Where all the bonds of death and hell are riven,
And mortal puts on immortality;
When Mercy's hand hath turned the Golden Key,
And Mercy's voice hath said, "Rejoice, Thy soul is
    free."

Harriet Beecher Stowe (1811-1896), from *Uncle Tom,'s Cabin*

BE STILL MY SOUL

Be still my soul: The Lord is on thy side;
With patience bear thy cross of grief or pain.
Leave to thy God to order and provide;
In every change he faithful will remain.
Be still my soul: Thy best thy heav'nly Friend
Thru thorny ways leads to a joyful end.

Be still my soul: Thy God doth undertake
To guide the future as he hath the past.
Thy hope, thy confidence let nothing shake;
All now mysterious shall be bright at last.
Be still my soul: the waves and winds still know
His voice who ruled them while he dwelt below.

Be still my soul: The hour is hast'ning on
When we shall be forever with the Lord,
When disappointment, grief and fear are gone,
Sorrow forgot, love's purest joys restored.
Be still my soul: When changes and tears are past,
All safe and blessed we shall meet at last.

Katharina von Schlegel (1697-) Translated by Jane Borthwick (1813-1897)

SERMONS

Some keep the Sabbath going to church;
I keep it staying at home,
With a bobolink for a chorister,
And an orchard for a dome.

Some keep the Sabbath in surplice;
I just wear my wings,
And instead of tolling the bell for church,
Our little sexton sings.

God preaches,—a noted clergyman,—
And the sermon is never long;
So instead of getting to heaven at last,
I'm going all along!

Emily Dickinson (1830-1886)

STORY OF GOD

I think when I read that sweet story of old,
When Jesus was here among men,
How he called little children like lambs to his fold:
I should like to have been with him then.

I wish that his hands had been placed on my head,
That his arms had been thrown around me,
That I might have seen his kind look when he said,
Let the little ones come unto me.

Yet still to my footstool in prayer I may go,
And ask for a share in his love;
And if I thus earnestly seek him below,
I shall see him and hear Him above.

Jemima Luke

CHARTLESS

I never saw a moor,
I never saw the sea;
Yet know I how the heather looks,
And what a wave must be.

I never spoke with God,
Nor visited in heaven;
Yet certain am I of the spot
As if the chart were given.

Emily Dickinson (1830-1886)

PRAYER TO PERSEPHONE

Be to her, Persephone,
All the things I might not be;
Take her head upon your knee.
She that was so proud and wild,
Flippant, arrogant and free,
She that had no need of me,
Is a little lonely child
Lost in Hell.—Persephone,
Take her head upon your knee;
Say to her, "My dear, my dear,
It is not so dreadful here."

Edna St. Vincent Millay (1892-1950)

BELIEF

'Twas God the word that spake it,
He took the bread and brake it;
And what the word did make it,
That I believe, and take it.

Elizabeth I, Queen of England (1533-1603)

GOODLY LAND

Oh, where is weeping Mary?
  Oh, where is weeping Mary?
  'Rived in the goodly land.
She is dead and gone to heaven;
  'Rived in the goodly land.
Oh, where are Paul and Silas?
  Oh, where are Paul and Silas?
  Gone to the goodly land.
They are dead and gone to heaven;
They are dead and gone to heaven;
  'Rived in the goodly land.

Negro spiritual, as recorded by Harriet Beecher Stowe
in *Uncle Tom's Cabin*

BECAUSE I HAVE BEEN GIVEN MUCH

Because I have been given much, I too must give;
Because of thy great bounty, Lord, each day I live
I shall divide my gifts from Thee With every brother that I
  see
Who has the need of help from me.

Because I have been sheltered, fed by thy good care,
I cannot see another's lack and I not share
My glowing fire, my loaf of bread, My roof's safe shelter
  over head,
That he too may be comforted.

Because I have been blessed by thy great love, dear Lord,
I'll share thy love again, according to thy word.
I shall give love to those in need; I'll show that love by
  word and deed:
Thus shall my thanks be thanks indeed.

Grace Noll Crowell (1877-1969)

OBERAMMERGAU

Rich man, poor man, beggar-man, thief,
Over the hills to the mountain folk,
Doctor, lawyer, merchant, chief,
Across the world they find their way;
Christ will be crucified today.

Christ will be crowned, and we are here.
Villager, are there beds enough?
Soup and bread and pot of beer?
Weary gentile, Turk, and Jew,
Lord and peasant, and Christian too.

Who called His name? What was it spoke?
Perhaps I dreamed. Then my walls dreamed!
I saw them shaking as I woke;
The dawn turned silver harps, and there
The Star hung singing in the air.

"Rich man, rich man, drawing near,
Have you not heard of the needle's eye?
Beggar, whom do you follow here?
Did you give to the poor as he bade you do?
Proud sir, which of the thieves are you?

"Doctor, lawyer, whom do you seek?
Do you succor the needy and ask no fee?
Chief, will you turn the other cheek?
Merchant, there is a story grim
Of money-changers scourged by Him!"

The star leaned lower from the sky:
"Oh, men in holy orders dressed,
Hurrying so to see Him die,
Important, as becomes your creed,
Why bring you dogma for His need?"

The streets of Oberammergau
Are waking now, are crowding now;
The Star has fallen like a tear;
There is a tree with a waiting bough
Not far from here.

Rich man, poor man, beggar and thief,
Over the hills to the mountain folk,
Doctor, lawyer, merchant, chief,
Magdalene, Mary great with grief,
And Martha walking heavily.
Doubter—dreaming—which am I?
Lord, help thou mine unbelief!

Leonora Speyer (1872-1956)

THE ONLY NEWS I KNOW

The only news I know
Is bulletins all day
From immortality.

The only shows I see
Tomorrow and Today,
Perchance Eternity.

The only One I meet
Is God,—the only street,
Existence; this traversed

If other news there be,
Or admirabler show—
I'll tell it you.

Emily Dickinson (1830-1886)

THE FIGHT OF FAITH

[One of the victims of the persecuting Henry VIII., the author was burnt to death at Smithfield in 1546. The following was made and sung by her while a prisoner in Newgate.]

Like as the armed Knighte,
Appointed to the fielde,
With this world wil I fight,
And faith shal be my shilde.

Faith is that weapon stronge,
Which wil not faile at nede;
My foes therefore amonge,
Therewith wil I procede.

As it is had in strengthe,
And forceso f Christes waye,
It wil prevaile at lengthe,
Through all the devils saye *naye*.

Faithe of the fathers olde
Obtained right witness,
Which makes me verye bolde
To fear no worldes distress.

I now rejoice in harte,
And hope bides me do so;
For Christ wil take my part,
And ease me of my wo.

Thou sayst, Lord, whoso knocke,
To them wilt thou attende;
Undo, therefore, the locke,
And thy stronge power sende.

More enemies now I have
Than heeres upon my head;

Let them not me deprave,
But fight thou in my steade.

On thee my care I cast,
For all their cruell spight;
I set not by their hast,
For thou art my delight.

I am not she that list
My anker to let fall
For every drislinge mist;
My shippe's substancial.

Not oft I use to wright
In prose, nor yet in ryme;
Yet wil I shewe one sight,
That I sawe in my time.

I sawe a royall throne,
Where Justice shulde have sitte;
But in her steade was One
Of moody cruell witte.

Absorpt was rightwisness,
As by the raginge floude;
Sathan, in his excess
Sucte up the guiltlesse bloude.

Then thought I,—Jesus, Lorde,
When thou shalt judge us all,
Harde is it to recorde
On these men what will fall.

Yet, Lorde, I thee desire,
For that they doe to me,
Let them not taste the hire
Of their iniquitie.

Anee Askewe (1521-1546)

IDEALS

To live and let live, without clamor for distinction or recognition; to wait on divine Love; to write truth first on the tablet of one's own heart,—this is the sanity and perfection of living, and my human ideal.

Mary Baker Eddy (1821-1910)

I NEED THEE EVERY HOUR

I need thee every hour,
Most gracious Lord.
No tender voice like thine
Can peace afford.
I need thee every hour;
Stay thou nearby.
Temptations lose their pow'r
When thou art nigh.

I need thee every hour,
In joy or pain.
Come quickly and abide,
Or life is vain.
I need thee every hour,
Most holy One.
Oh, make me thine indeed,
Thou blessed Son.

Refrain

I need thee, oh, I need thee,
Every hour I need thee!
Oh bless me now, my Savior;
I come to thee!

Annie S. Hawkes (1835-1918)

GREAT KING OF HEAVEN

Great King of heav'n, our hearts we raise
To thee in prayer, to thee in praise.
The vales exult, the hills acclaim,
And all thy works revere thy name.

O Israel's God! Thine arm is strong.
To thee all earth and skies belong,
And with one voice in one glad chord,
With myriad echoes, praise the Lord.

Carrie Stockdale Thomas (1848-1931)

HOW GREAT THE WISDOM AND THE LOVE

How great the wisdom and the love
    That filled the courts on high,
And sent the Savior from above
    To suffer, bleed, and die!

His precious blood he freely spilt;
    His life he freely gave,
A sinless sacrifice for guilt,
    A dying world to save.

By strict obedience Jesus won
    The prize with glory rife:
"Thy will, O God, not mine be done,"
    Adorned his mortal life.

He marked the path and led the way,
    And ev'ry point defines
To light and life and endless day
    Where God's full presence shines.

Eliza R. Snow (1804-1887)

MASTER, THE TEMPEST IS RAGING

Master, the tempest is raging!
The billows are tossing high!
The sky is o'er-shadowed with blackness.
No shelter or help is nigh.
Carest thou not that we perish?
How canst thou lie asleep
When each moment so madly is threat'ning
A grave in the angry deep?

Master, with anguish of spirit
I bow in my grief today.
The depths of my sad heart are troubled.
Oh, waken and save, I pray!
Torrents of sin and of anguish
Sweep o'er my sinking soul,
And I perish! I perish! dear Master.
Oh, hasten and take control!

Master, the terror is over.
The elements sweetly rest.
Earth's sun in the calm lake is mirrored,
And heaven's within my breast.
Linger, O blessed Redeemer!
Leave me alone no more,
And with joy I shall make the blest harbor
And rest on the blissful shore.

Refrain

The winds and the waves shall obey thy will:
    Peace, be still.
Whether the wrath of the storm-tossed sea
Or demons or men or whatever it be,
No waters can swallow the ship where lies
The Master of ocean and earth and skies.

They all shall sweetly obey thy will:
    Peace, be still; Peace, be still.
They all shall sweetly obey thy will:
    Peace, peace, be still.

Mary Ann Baker (ca.1874)

DID YOU THINK TO PRAY?

Ere you left your room this morning,
Did you think to pray?
In the name of Christ our Savior,
Did you sue for loving favor
As a shield today?

When your heart was filled with anger,
Did you think to pray?
Did you plead for grace, my brother,
That you might forgive another
Who had crossed your way?

When sore trials came upon you,
Did you think to pray?
When your soul was full of sorrow,
Balm of Gilead did you borrow
At the gates of day?

Refrain

Oh, how praying rests the weary!
Prayer will change the night to day.
So, when life gets dark and dreary,
Don't forget to pray.

Mary A. Pepper Kidder (1820-1905)

NATURE

Being is holiness, harmony, immortality. It is already proved that a knowledge of this, even in a small degree, will uplift the physical and moral standards of mortals, will increase longevity, will purify and elevate character. Thus progress will finally destroy all error, and bring immortality to light.

Mary Baker Eddy (1821-1910)

THIS VERY HOUR

Master, this very hour,
  Under this village sky,
Between two thieves You go,
  To die.

About our separate work,
  Ever we come and pass;
One Pilate; Andrew one;
  One scarlet Caiaphas.

Peter stoops to his bulbs,
  Under a kitchen pane;
And James halts there to talk
  Of day's luck, field or rain.

Along some brambly wall,
  Where orange haws burn hot,
His thirty coins held fast,
  Goes dark Iscariot.

Lizette Woodworth Reese (1856-1935)

Jesus loves me—this I know,
For the Bible tells me so.

Anna Bartlett Warner (1827-1915)
from *The Love of Jesus*

GREAT GOD, TO THEE MY EVENING SONG

Great God, to thee my evening song
    With humble gratitude I raise;
Oh, let thy mercy tune my tongue
    And fill my heart with praise.

My days, unclouded as they pass,
    And ev'ry onward rolling hour
Are monuments of wondrous grace,
    And witness to thy love and pow'r.

With hope in thee my eyelids close;
    With sleep refresh my feeble frame.
Safe in thy care may I repose
    And wake with praises to thy name.

Anne Steel (1716-1778)

CHILDREN OF OUR HEAVENLY FATHER

Children of our Heavenly Father
Safely in his bosom gather;
Nestling bird nor star in heaven
Such a refuge e'er was given.

Neither life nor death shall ever
From the Lord his children sever;
Unto them his grace he showeth,
And their sorrows all he knoweth.

Though he giveth or he taketh,
God his children ne'er forsaketh;
His the loving purpose solely
To preserve them pure and holy.

Caroline V. Sandell-Berg (1832-1903), trans. by Ernst W. Olson

THE NEW EZEKIEL

What, can these dead bones live, whose sap is dried
   By twenty scorching centuries of wrong?
Is this the House of Israel, whose pride
   Is as a tale that's told, an ancient song?
Are these ignoble relics all that live
   Of psalmist, priest, and prophet? Can the breath
Of very heaven bid these bones revive,
   Open the graves and clothe the ribs of death?
Yea, Prophesy, the Lord hath said. Again
   Say to the wind, Come forth and breathe afresh,
Even that they may live upon these slain,
   And bone to bone shall leap, and flesh to flesh.
The spirit is not dead, proclaims the word,
   Where lay dead bones, a host of armed men
stand!
I ope your graves, my people, saith the Lord,
   And I shall place you living in your land.

          Emma Lazarus (1849-1887)

GOD'S WILL

   Be not afraid, ye waiting hearts that weep,
   For God still giveth His beloved sleep,
   And if an endless sleep He wills—so best.

          Henrietta A. Heathhorn (1825-1914)

PRAISE

   "Praise God from whom all blessings flow,"
   Praise him who sendeth joy and woe
   The Lord who takes, the Lord who gives,
   O praise him, all that dies, and lives.

          Dinah Marie Mulock Craik (1826-1887)

NEARER HOME

One sweetly solemn thought
   Comes to me o'er and o'er;
I am nearer home to-day
   Than I have ever been before;

Nearer my Father's house,
   Where the many mansions be;
Nearer the great white throne,
   Nearer the crystal sea;

Nearer the bound of life,
   Where we lay our burdens down;
Nearer leaving the cross,
   Nearer gaining the crown!

But lying darkly between,
   Winding down through the night,
Is the silent, unknown stream,
   That leads at last to the light.

Closer and closer my steps
   Come to the dread abysm:
Closer death to my lips
   Passes the awful chrism.

Oh, if my mortal feet
   Have almost gained the brink;
If it be I am nearer home
   Even today than I think;

Father, perfect my trust;
   Let my spirit feel in death,
That her feet are warmly set
   On the rock of a living faith!

Phoebe Cary (1824-1871)

THE CHOIR INVISIBLE

Oh, may I join the choir invisible
Of those immortal dead who live again
In minds made better by their presence; live
In pulses stirred to generosity,
In deeds of daring rectitude, in scorn
For miserable aims that end with self,
In thoughts sublime that pierce the night like stars,
And with their mild persistence urge men's search
To vaster issues. So to live in heaven:
To make undying music in the world,
Breathing a beauteous order that controls
With growing sway the growing life of man.
So we inherit that sweet purity
For which we struggled, failed, and agonized
With widening retrospect that bred despair.
Rebellious flesh that would not be subdued,
A vicious parent shaming still its child,
Poor anxious penitence, is quick dissolved;
Its discords, quenched by meeting harmonies,
Die in the large and charitable air.
And all our rarer, better, truer self,
That sobbed religiously in yearning song,
That watched to ease the burden of the world,
Laboriously tracing what must be,
And what may yet be better,—saw within
A worthier image for the sanctuary,
And shaped it forth before the multitude,
Divinely human, raising worship so
To higher reverence more mixed with love,—
That better self shall live till human Time
Shall fold its eyelids, and the human sky
Be gathered like a scroll within the tomb
Unread forever. This is life to come,—
Which martyred men have made more glorious
For us who strive to follow. May I reach

That purest heaven,—be to other souls
The cup of strength in some great agony,
Enkindle generous ardor, feed pure love,
Beget the smiles that have no cruelty,
Be the sweet presence of a good diffused,
And in diffusion ever more intense!
So shall I join the choir invisible
Whose music is the gladness of the world.

George Eliot (1819-1880)

THE JUDGEMENT

Thou hast done evil
And given place to the devil;
Yet so cunningly thou concealest
The thing which thou feelest,
That no eye espieth it,
Satan himself denieth it.
Go where it chooseth thee;
Neither foe nor lover
Will the wrong uncover;
The world's breath raiseth thee.
And thy own past praiseth thee.
Yet know thou this:
At quick of thy being
Is an all eye seeing,
The snake's wit evadeth not;
The charmed lip persuadeth not;
So thoroughly it despiseth
The thing thy hand prizeth
Though the sun were thy clothing,
It should count thee for nothing.
Thine own eye divineth thee,
Thine own soul arraigneth thee;
God himself cannot shrive thee
Till that judge forgive thee.

Dora Read Goodale (1866-   )

THE COMMON STREET

The common street climbed up against the sky,
Gray meeting gray; and wearily to and fro
I saw the patient common people go,
Each, with his sordid burden, trudging by.
And the rain dropped; there was not any sigh
Or stir of a live wind; dull, dull and slow
All motion; as a tale told long ago
The faded world; and creeping night drew nigh.

Then burst the sunset, flooding far and fleet,
Leavening the whole of life with magic leaven.
Suddenly down the long wet glistening hill
Pure splendor poured—and lo! the common street,
A golden highway into golden heaven,
With the dark shapes of men ascending still.

Helen Gray Cone (1859-1934)

GOD, OUR FATHER, HEAR US PRAY

God, our Father, hear us pray;
    Send thy grace this holy day.
As we take of emblems blest,
    On our Savior's love we rest.

Grant us, Father, thy grace divine;
    May thy smile upon us shine.
As we eat the broken bread,
    Thine approval on us shed.

As we drink the water clear,
    Let thy Spirit linger near.
Pardon faults, O Lord, we pray;
    Bless our efforts day by day.

Annie Pincock Malin (1863-1935)

GREAT IS THE LORD

Great is the Lord; 'tis good to praise
His high and holy name.
Well may the Saints in latter days
His wondrous love proclaim.

The Comforter is sent again;
His pow'r the Church attends,
And with the faithful will remain
Till Jesus Christ descends.

We'll praise him for a prophet's voice,
His people's steps to guide;
In this we do and will rejoice,
Tho all the world deride.

To praise him let us all engage,
For unto us is giv'n
To live in this momentous age
And share the light of heaven.

Eliza R. Snow (1804-1887)

AT LAST

When sinks the soul, subdued by toil to slumber,
Its closing eyes look up to thee in prayer,
Sweet the repose beneath thy wings o'ershading
But sweeter still to wake and find thee there.

So shall it be at last in that bright morning
When the soul waketh, and life's shadows flee,
O in that hour, fairer than daylight's dawning,
Shall rise the glorious thought, I am with thee—
Still, still with thee.

Harriet Beecher Stowe (1811-1896)

COMRADE JESUS

Thanks to St. Matthew, who had been
At mass-meetings in Palestine,
We know whose side was spoken for
When comrade Jesus had the floor.

"Where sore they toil and hard they lie,
Among the great unwashed am I.—
The tramp, the convict, I am he;
Cold-shoulder him, cold-shoulder me."

By Dives' door, with thoughtful eye,
He did tomorrow prophesy:—
"The Kingdom's gate is low and small;
The rich can scarce wedge through at all."

"A dangerous man," said Caiaphas,
"An ignorant demagogue, alas!
Friend of low women, it is he
Slanders the upright Pharisee."

For law and order it was plain,
For Holy Church, he must be slain.
The troops were there to awe the crowd:
Mob violence was not allowed.

Their clumsy force with force to foil
His strong, clean hands he would not soil.
He saw their childishness quite plain
Between the lightnings of his pain.

Between the twilights of his end,
He made his fellow-felon friend:
With swollen tongue and blinded eyes,
Invited him to Paradise.

Ah, let no local him refuse!
Comrade Jesus has paid his due.
Whatever other be debarred,
Comrade Jesus hath his red card.

Sarah Norcliffe Cleghorn (1876-1959)

IN HYMNS OF PRAISE

In hymns of praise your voices raise
    To him who reigns on high,
Whose counsels keep the mighty deep,
    Who ruleth earth and sky.

Beneath his hand at his command,
    The shining planets move;
To all below they daily show
    His wisdom and his love.

The little flow'r that lasts an hour,
    The sparrow in its fall,
They, too, shall share his tender care;
    He made and loves them.

Then sing again in lofty strain
    To him who dwells on high;
To prayers you raise, and songs of praise,
    He sweetly will reply.

Refrain

Exalt his name in loud acclaim;
His mighty pow'r adore!
And humbly bow before him now,
Our King forever more.

Ada Blenkhorn

GOD REST YE, MERRY GENTLEMEN

God rest ye, merry gentlemen,
Let nothing you dismay,
Remember Christ our Savior
Was born on Christmas Day,
To save us all from Satan's pow'r
When we were gone astray;

In Bethlehem, in Jewry,
This blessed Babe was born,
And laid within a manger,
Upon this holy morn
The which His Mother Mary,
Did nothing take in scorn.

From God our Heavenly Father
A blessed angel came;
And unto certain Shepherds
Brought tidings of the same:
How that in Bethlehem was born
The son of God by name.

"Fear not then," said the Angel
"Let nothing you affright,
This day is born a Savior
Of a pure Virgin bright,
To free all those who trust in Him
From Satan's power and might."

The shepherds at those tidings
Rejoiced much in mind,
And left their flocks a-feeding,
In tempest, storm, and wind:
And went to Bethlehem straightway,
The Son of God to find.

And when they came to Bethlehem
Where our dear Savior lay,
They found him in a manger,
Where oxen feed on hay;
His Mother Mary kneeling down,
Unto the Lord did pray.

Now to the Lord sing praises,
All you within this place,
And with true love and brotherhood
Each other now embrace;
This holy tide of Christmas
All other doth deface.

Dinah Maria Mulock Craik (1826-1887)

A CHILD'S THOUGHT OF GOD

They say that God lives very high!
    But if you look above the pines
You cannot see our God. And why?

And if you dig down in the mines
    You never see Him in the gold,
Though from Him all that's glory shines.

God is so good, He wears a fold
    Of heaven and earth across His face—
Like secrets kept, for love untold.

But still I feel that His embrace
    Slides down by thrills, through all things made,
Through sight and sound of every place:

As if my tender mother laid
    On my shut lids her kisses pressure,
Half-waking me at night and said,
    "Who kissed you through the dark, dear guesser?"

Elizabeth Barrettt Browning (1806-1861)

BEHOLD! A ROYAL ARMY

Behold a royal army,
　　With banner, sword, and shield,
Is marching forth to conquer
　　On life's great battle field.
Its ranks are filled with soldiers,
　　United bold and strong,
Who follow their commander
　　And sing their joyful song:

And now the foe advancing,
　　That valiant host assails,
And yet they never falter;
　　Their courage never fails.
Their leader calls, "Be faithful!"
　　They pass the word along;
They see his signal flashing
　　And shout their joyful song:

Oh, when the war is ended,
　　When strife and conflicts cease,
When all are safely gathered
　　Within the vale of peace,
Before the king eternal,
　　That vast and mighty throng
Shall praise his name forever,
　　And this shall be their song:

Refrain

Victory, victory, Through him that redeemed
us!
Victory, victory, Through Jesus Christ, our
Lord!
Victory, victory, victory,
Through Jesus Christ our Lord!

Fanny J. Crosby (1820-1915)

O MY FATHER

O my Father, thou that dwellest
In the high and glorious place,
When shall I regain thy presence
And again behold thy face?
In thy holy habitation,
Did my spirit once reside?
In my first primeval childhood,
Was I nurtured by thy side?

For a wise and glorious purpose
Thou hast placed me here on earth
And withheld the recollection
Of my former friends and birth;
Yet ofttimes a secret something
Whispered, "You're a stranger here,"
I felt that I had wandered
From a more exalted sphere.

I had learned to call thee Father,
Through thy spirit from on high,
But, until the key of knowledge
Was restored, I know not why.
In the heavens are parents single?
No, the thought makes reason stare!
Truth is reason; truth eternal
Tells me I've a mother there.

When I leave this frail existence,
When I lay this mortal by,
Father, Mother, may I meet you
In your royal courts on high?
Then, at length, when I've completed
All you sent me forth to do,
With your mutual approbation
Let me come and dwell with you.

Eliza R. Snow (1804-1887)

SCATTER SUNSHINE

In a world where sorrow
    Ever will be known,
Where are found the needy
    And the sad and lone,
How much joy and comfort
    You can all bestow,
If you scatter sunshine
    Everywhere you go.

Slightest actions often
    Meet the sorest needs,
For the world wants daily
    Little kindly deeds.
Oh, what care and sorrow
    You may help remove,
With your songs and courage,
    Sympathy and love.

When the days are gloomy,
    Sing some happy song;
Meet the world's repining
    With a courage strong.
Go with faith undaunted
    Thru the ills of life;
Scatter smiles and sunshine
    O'er its toil and strife.

Refrain

Scatter sunshine all along your way.
Cheer and bless and brighten.
Every passing day.

                                          Lanta Wilson Smith

NEARER, MY GOD, TO THEE

Nearer, my God, to Thee,
Nearer to Thee!
E'en though it be a cross
That raiseth me;
Still all my song shall be,
Nearer, my God, to Thee,
Nearer to Thee!

Though like the wanderer,
The sun gone down,
Darkness be over me,
My rest a stone;
Yet in my dreams I'd be
Nearer, my God, to Thee,
Nearer to Thee!

There let the way appear
Steps unto Heaven,
All that Thou send'st me
In mercy given;
Angels to beckon me
Nearer, my God, to Thee,
Nearer to Thee!

Then, with my waking thoughts
Bright with Thy praise,
Out of my stony griefs,
Bethel I'll raise;
So by my woes to be
Nearer, my God, to Thee,
Nearer to Thee!

Or if, on joyful wing,
Cleaving the sky,
Sun, moon and stars forgot,

Upward I fly,
Still all my song shall be,
Nearer, my God to Thee,
Nearer to Thee!

Sarah Flower Adams (1805-1848)

DEAR TO THE HEART OF THE SHEPHERD

Dear to the heart of the shepherd,
    Dear are the sheep of his fold;
Dear is the love that he gives them,
    Dearer than silver or gold.
Dear to the heart of the shepherd,
    Dear are the "other" lost sheep;
Over the mountains he follows,
    Over the waters so deep.

Dear to the heart of the shepherd,
    Dear are the lambs of his fold;
Some from the pastures are straying,
    Hungry and helpless and cold.
See, the Good Shepherd, is seeking,
    Seeking the lambs that are lost,
Bringing them in with rejoicing,
    Saved at such infinite cost.

Dear to the heart of the shepherd,
    Dear are the "ninety and nine;"
Dear are the sheep that have wandered
    Out in the desert to pine.
Hark! He is earnestly calling,
    Tenderly pleading today:
"Will you not seek for the lost ones,
    Off from my shelter astray?"

Green are the pastures inviting;
    Sweet are the waters and still.
Lord, we will answer thee gladly,
    "Yes, blessed Master, we will!"
Make us thy true under-shepherds;
    Give us a love that is deep.
Send us out into the desert,
    Seeking thy wandering sheep."

Refrain

Out in the desert they wander,
Hungry and helpless and cold;
Off to the rescue he hastens,
Bringing them back to the fold.

Mary B. Wingate (1899-   )

HAPPINESS

Faith that withstood the shocks of toil and time;
    Hope that defied despair;
    Patience that conquered care;
And loyalty, whose courage was sublime;
The great deep heart that was a home for all,—
    Just, eloquent, and strong
    In protest against wrong;
Wide charity, that knew no sin, no fall;
The Spartan spirit that made life so grand,
    Mating poor daily needs
    With high, heroic deeds,
That wrested happiness from Fate's hard hands.

Louisa May Alcott (1832-1888)

One sweetly solemn thought
Comes to me o'er and o'er;
I am nearer home today
Than I ever have been before.

Phoebe Cary (1824-1871)

WHO'S ON THE LORD'S SIDE?

Who's on the Lord's side? Who?
Now is the time to show.
We ask it fearlessly:
Who's on the Lord's side? Who?
We wage no common war,
Cope with no common foe.
The enemy's awake;
Who's on the Lord's side? Who?

We serve the living God,
And want his foes to know
That, if but few, we're great;
Who's on the Lord's side? Who?
We're going on to win;
No fear must blanch the brow.
The Lord of Hosts is ours;
Who's on the Lord's side? Who?

The stone cut without hands
To fill the earth must grow.
Who'll help to roll it on?
Who's on the Lord's side? Who?
Our ensign to the world
Is floating proudly now.
No coward bears our flag;
Who's on the Lord's side? Who?

The pow'rs of earth and hell
In rage direct the blow
That's aimed to crush the work;
Who's on the Lord's side? Who?
Truth, life, and liberty,
Freedom from death and woe,
Are stakes we're fighting for;
Who's on the Lord's side? Who?

Hannah Last Cornaby (1822-1905)

FOR THE STRENGTH OF THE HILLS

For the strength of the hills we bless thee,
Our God, our fathers' God;
Thou hast made thy children mighty
By the touch of the mountain sod.
Thou hast led thy chosen Israel
To freedom's last abode;
For the strength of the hills we bless thee,
Our God, our fathers' God.

At the hands of foul oppressors,
We've borne and suffered long;
Thou hast been our help in weakness,
And thy pow'r hath made us strong.
Amid ruthless foes outnumbered,
In weariness we trod;
For the strength of the hills we bless thee,
Our God, our fathers' God.

Thou hast led us here in safety
Where the mountain bulwark stands
As the guardian of the loved ones
Thou has brought from many lands.
For the rock and for the river,
The valley's fertile sod,
For the strength of the hills we bless thee,
Our God, our fathers' God.

We are watchers of a beacon
Whose light must never die;
We are guardians of an altar
'Midst the silence of the sky.
Here the rocks yield founts of courage,
Struck forth as by thy rod;
For the strength of the hills we bless thee,
Our God, our fathers' God.

Felicia Dorothea Hemans (1793-1835)

I AM A CHILD OF GOD

I am a child of God,
And he has sent me here,
Has given me an earthly home
With parents kind and dear.
Lead me, guide me, walk beside me,
Help me find the way.
Teach me all that I must do
to live with him some-day.

I am a child of God,
And so my needs are great;
Help me to understand his words
Before it grows too late.
Lead me, guide me, walk beside me,
Help me find the way.
Teach me all that I must do
To live with him some-day.

I am a child of God.
Rich blessings are in store;
If I but learn to do his will
I'll live with him once more.
Lead me, guide me, walk beside me,
Help me find the way.
Teach me all that I must do
To live with him some-day.

Naomi W. Randall (1908-   )
"I am a Child of God" © 1957 by The Church of
Jesus Christ of Latter-day Saints. Used by permission.

GODLY

And when, the tempest passing by,
He gleams out, sunlike, through our sky,
We look up, and through black clouds riven
We recognize the smile of Heaven.

Diana Marie Mulock Craik (1826-1887)

TRUTH REFLECTS UPON OUR SENSES

Truth reflects upon our senses;
Gospel light reveals to some.
If there still should be offenses,
Woe to them by whom they come!
Judge not, that ye be not judged,
Was the counsel Jesus gave;
Measure given, large or grudged,
Just the same you must receive.

(Chorus)
Blessed Savior, thou wilt guide us,
Till we reach that blissful shore
Where the angels wait to join us
In thy praise forever more.

Jesus said, "Be meek and lowly,"
For 'tis high to be a judge;
If I would be pure and holy,
I must love without a grudge.
It requires a constant labor
All his precepts to obey.
If I truly love my neighbor,
I am in the narrow way.
(Chorus)

Once I said unto another,
"In thine eye there is a mote;
If thou art a friend, a brother,
Hold, and let me pull it out."
But I could not see it fairly,
For my sight was very dim.
When I came to search more clearly,
In mine eye there was a beam.
(Chorus)

Eliza R. Snow (1804-1887)

LOVE ONE ANOTHER

As I have loved you,
Love one another.
This new commandment:
Love one another.
By this shall men know
Ye are my disciples,
If ye have love
One to another.

Luacine Clark Fox (1914-   )

IN OUR LOVELY DESERET

In our lovely Deseret,
Where the Saints of God have met,
There's a multitude of children all around.
They are generous and brave;
They have precious souls to save;
They must listen and obey the gospel's sound.

(Chorus)
Hark! hark! hark! 'tis children's music—
Children's voices, oh, how sweet,
When in innocence and love,
Like the angels up above,
They with happy hearts and cheerful faces meet.

That the children may live long
And be beautiful and strong,
Tea and coffee and tobacco they despise,
Drink no liquor, and they eat
But a very little meat;
They are seeking to be great and good and wise.
(Chorus)

They should be instructed young
How to watch and guard the tongue,
And their tempers train and evil passions bind;
They should always be polite,
And treat ev'rybody right,
And in ev'ry place be affable and kind.
(Chorus)

They must not forget to pray,
Night and morning ev'ry day,
For the Lord to keep them safe from ev'ry ill,
And assist them to do right,
That with all their mind and might,
They may love him and may learn to do his will.
(Chorus)

Eliza R. Snow (1804-1887)

LET IT BE FORGOTTEN

Let it be forgotten, as a flower is forgotten,
    Forgotten as a fire that once was singing gold,
Let it be forgotten for ever and ever,
    Time is a kind friend, he will make us old.

If anyone asks, say it was forgotten
    Long and long ago,
As a flower, as a fire, as a hushed footfall
    In a long-forgotten snow.

Sarah Teasdale (1884-1933)

I watched the hills drank the last color of light,
All shapes grow bright and wane on the pale air,
Till down the traitorous east there came the night,
And swept the circle of my seeing bare.

Leonie Adams (1899-   )

A DOUBTING HEART

Where are the swallows fled?
        Frozen and dead
Perchance upon some bleak and stormy shore.
        O doubting heart!
    Far over purple seas
    They wait, in sunny ease,
    The balmy southern breeze
To bring them to their northern homes once more.

Why must the flowers die?
        Prisoned they lie
In the cold tomb, heedless of tears or rain.
        O doubting heart!
    They only sleep below
    The soft white ermine snow
    While winter winds shall blow,
To breathe and smile upon you soon again.

The sun has hid its rays
        These many days;
Will dreary hours never leave the earth?
        O doubting heart!
    The stormy clouds on high
    Veil the same sunny sky
    That soon, for spirng is nigh,
Shall wake the summer into golden mirth.

Fair hope is dead, and light
        Is quenched in night;
What sound can break the silence of despair?
        O doubting heart!
    The sky is overcast,
    Yet stars shall rise at last,
    Brighter for darkness past,
And angels' silver voices stir the air.

Adelaide Anne Procter (1825-1864)

5

TRIBUTES TO WOMEN BY MEN

SPHERE OF WOMEN

They talk about a woman's sphere as though it had a limit;
There's not a place in Earth or Heaven,
There's not a task to mankind given,
There's not a blessing or a woe,
There's not a whispered yes or no,
There's not a life, or death, or birth,
That has a feather's weight or worth—
Without a woman in it.

C. E. Bowman (c. 1905)

Victory of Samothrace
Circa 190 B.C. Discovered in Samothrace in 1863.

The Madonna of Goldfinch
Raphael (1483-1520)

Portrait of Mona Lisa
Leonardo Da Vinci (1452-1519)

"Back From Market"
Jean-Batpiste Simeon Chardin (1699-1779)

Statue of Liberty
Frederic Augustes Bartholdi (1834-1904)

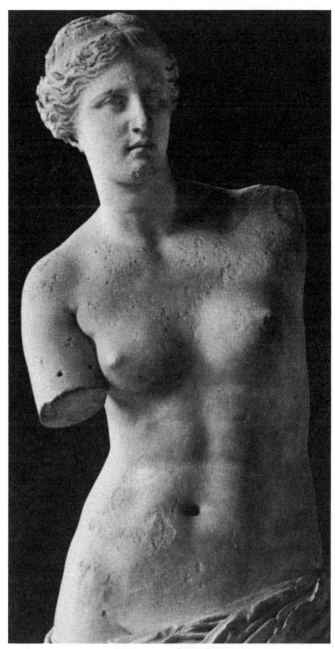

Venus of Milos
Second half of 11th Century B.C.
Found on the Island of Milos, 1820.

I PRITHEE SEND ME BACK MY HEART

I prithee send me back my heart,
     Since I cannot have thine;
For if from yours you will not part,
     Why then shouldst thou have mine?

Yet, now I think on't, let it lie;
     To find it were in vain;
For thou'st a thief in either eye
     Would steal it back again.

Why should two hearts in one breast lie,
     And yet not lodge together?
O Love! where is thy sympathy
     If thus our breasts thou sever?

But love is such a mystery,
     I cannot find it out;
For when I think I'm best resolved
     Then I am most in doubt.

Then farewell care, and farewell woe;
     I will no longer pine;
For I'll believe I have her heart
     As much as she has mine.

                              Sir John Suckling (1609-1641)

A VISION OF BEAUTY

It was a beauty that I saw,—
     So pure, so perfect, as the frame
     Of all the universe were lame
To that one figure, could I draw,
Or give least line of it a law:
     A skein of silk without a knot!
A fair march made without a halt!

A curious form without a fault!
    A printed book without a blot!
    All beauty!—and without a spot.

Ben Jonson (1573-1637)

LOVE-LETTERS IN FLOWERS

"An exquisite invention this,
Worthy of Love's most honeyed kiss,—
This art of writing billet-doux
In buds, and odors, and bright hues!"

JENNY KISSED ME

Jenny kissed me when we met,
    Jumping from the chair she sat in.
Time, you thief! who love to get
    Sweets into your list, put that in.
Say I'm weary, say I'm sad;
    Say that health and wealth have missed me;
Say I'm growing old , but add . . .
    Jenny kissed me!

James Henry Leigh Hunt (1774-1859)

LOVE'S POWER

I never knew a night so black
Light failed to follow on its track.
I never knew a storm so grey
It failed to have a clearing day.
I never knew such bleak despair
That there was not a rift somewhere.
I never knew an hour so drear
Love could not fill it full of cheer.

John K. Bangs (1882-1922)

ANNIE LAURIE

Max-welton braes are bonnie,
Where early fa's the dew,
And it's there that Annie Laurie,
Gie'd me her promise true,
Gie'd me her promise true,
Which ne'er forgot will be;
And for bonnie Annie Laurie
I'd lay me down and dee.

Her brow is like the snaw-drift,
Her throat is like the swan,
Her face, it is the fairest,
That e'er the sun shone on,
That e'er the sun shone on;
And dark blue is her e'e,
And for bonnie Annie Laurie
I'd lay me down and dee.

Like dew on the gowan lying
Is the fa' o' her fairy feet,
Winds in summer sighing,
Her voice is low and sweet,
Her voice is low and sweet;
She's a' the world to me,
And for bonnie Annie Lauire
I'd lay me down and dee.

Unknown male author

VIRTUOUS WOMAN

Who can find a virtuous woman? for her price *is* far above
rubies. The heart of her husband doth safely trust in her, so
that he shall have no need of spoil. She will do him good and
not evil all the days of her life. She seeketh wool, and flax,
and worketh willingly with her hands. She is like the
merchants' ships; she bringeth her food from afar.

Proverbs 31:10-14

BELIEVE ME, IF ALL THOSE
ENDEARING YOUNG CHARMS

Believe me, if all those endearing young charms
    Which I gaze on so fondly today,
Were to change by tomorrow, and fleet in my arms,
    Like fairy gifts fading away,
Thou would'st still be adored, as the moment thou art,
    Let thy loveliness fade as it will,
And around the dear ru-in each wish of my heart,
    Would entwine itself verdantly still.

It is not while beauty and youth are thine own,
    And thy cheeks unprofaned by a tear,
That the fervor and faith of a soul can be known,
    To which time will but make thee more dear.
No, the heart that has truly loved never forgets,
    But as truly loves on to the close,
And as the sun-flower turns on her god, when he sets,
    The same look which she turn'd when he rose.

Thomas Moore (1779-1852)

MY LADY WALKS IN LOVELINESS

My lady walks in loveliness
And shames the moon's cold grace.
A thousand songs dwell in her voice,
A thousand songs dwell in her voice,
Enchantment in her face,
And Love, himself, lays down his lute
To mark her passing there,
A lovely lyric-lady
With sunset in her hair,
With sunset in her hair.

Ernest Charles

OH I HAD SUCH A PRETTY DREAM MAMMA

Oh, I had such a pretty dream, Mamma,
  Such pleasant and beautiful things;
Of a dear little nest, in the meadows of rest,
  Where the birdie her lullaby sings.
Of a dear little nest, in the meadows of rest,
  Where the birdie her lullaby sings.

A dear little stream full of lilies,
  Crept over the green mossy stones,
And just where I lay, its thin sparkling spray
  Sang sweetly in delicate tones.
And just where I lay, its thin sparkling spray
  Sang sweetly in delicate tones.

And as it flowed on toward the ocean,
  Thro' shadows and pretty sunbeams,
Each note grew more deep, and I soon fell asleep,
  And was off to the Island of Dreams.
Each note grew more deep, and I soon fell asleep,
  And was off to the Island of Dreams.

I saw there a beautiful angel,
  With crown all bespangled with dew:
She touched me, and spoke, and I quickly awoke;
  And found there, dear mamma, 'twas you.
She touched me, and spoke, and I quickly awoke:
  And found thre, dear mamma, 'twas you.

Unknown

Although the author of this beautiful poem is not specifically known to be a male I am including it under Tributes, anyway, because of its nostalgic and inspirational message to each of us.

Sidney S. Smith

MY BONNIE

My Bonnie lies over the ocean,
My Bonnie lies over the sea,
My Bonnie lies over the ocean,
Oh bring back my Bonnie to me.

Last night as I lay on my pillow,
Last night as I lay on my bed,
Last night as I lay on my pillow,
I dreamt that my Bonnie was dead.

O blow, ye winds, over the ocean,
O blow, ye winds, over the sea,
O blow, ye winds, over the ocean,
And bring back my Bonnie to me.

Refrain:

Bring back, bring back,
Bring back my Bonnie to me, to me;
Bring back, bring back,
Oh, bring back my Bonnie to me.

Unknown male author — Scottish Song

MATILDA

Here lies Henry's daughter, wife and mother . . .
Great by birth, Greater by marriage,
Greatest by Motherhood.

Epitaph of Matilda (1167); daughter of Henry I of England and Matilda, married Holy Roman Emperor Henry V, after his death married Geoffry Plantagenet, mother of Henry II of England in 1152, eight weeks after divorce from Louis VII; she had been imprisoned for fifteen years.

MY WILD IRISH ROSE

If you listen, I'll sing you a sweet little song
Of a flower that's now drooped and dead,
Yet—dearer to me, Yes, than all of its mates,
Tho' each holds aloft its proud head.

'Twas given to me by a girl that I know;
Since, we've met, faith, I've known no repose,
She is dearer by far than the world's brightest star,
And I call her my wild Irish rose.

They may sing of their roses which by other names,
Would smell just as sweetly, they say,
But I know that my Rose, would never consent
To have that sweet name taken away.

Her glances are shy whene'er I pass by
The bower where my true love grows.
And my one wish has been that some day I may win
The heart of my wild Irish rose.

Refrain:

My wild Irish rose,
The sweetest flower that grows,
You may search everywhere,
But none can compare
With my wild Irish rose.

My wild Irish rose,
The sweetest flower that grows,
You may search everywhere,
But none can compare
With my wild Irish rose.

My wild Irish rose,
The sweetest flower that grows,
And some day for my sake,
She may let me take
The bloom from my wild Irish rose.

Chauncey Olcott (1860-1932)

WEAKER SEX

To call women the weaker sex is a libel: it is man's injustice to women. If by strength is meant brute strength, then indeed, is woman less brute than man. If by strength is meant moral power, then woman is immeasurably man's superior. Has she not got greater powers of endurance, has she not greater courage? Without her man would not be. If nonviolence is the law of our being, the future is with women.

Mohandes Karamchand Gandhi (1869-1948)

WOMAN

As unto the bow the cord is,
So unto the man is woman;
Though she bends him, she obeys him,
Though she draws him, yet she follows;
Useless each without the other.

Henry Wadsworth Longfellow (1807-1882), from "Miles Standish"

I remember my mother's prayers and they have always followed me. They have clung to me all my life.

Abraham Lincoln (1809-1865)

GREETINGS

There is nothing I can give you which you have not got;
but there is much, very much, that, while I cannot give it,
you can take. No Heaven can come to us unless our hearts
find rest in it to-day. Take Heaven! No peace lies in the
future which is not hidden in this present little instant.
Take peace!

The gloom of the world is but a shadow. Behind it, yet
within our reach, is joy. There is radiance and glory in the
darkness, could we but see; and to see, we have only to
look. Contessina I beseech you to look.

Life is so generous a giver, but we, judging its gifts by
their covering, cast them away as ugly or heavy or hard.
Remove the covering, and you will find beneath it a living
splendour, woven of love, by wisdom, with power; Welcome it, grasp it, and you touch the Angel's hand that
brings it to you. Everything we call a trial, a sorrow, or a
duty: believe me, that angel's hand is there; the gift is
there, and the wonder of an overshadowing Presence. Our
joys, too: be not content with them as joys, they too con-
ceal diviner gifts.

Life is so full of meaning and of purpose, so full of
beauty—beneath its covering—that you will find that
earth but cloaks your heaven. Courage, then to claim it:
that is all! But courage you have; and the knowledge that
we are pilgrims together, wending through unknown country, home.

And so, at this Christmas time, I greet you; not quite as
the world sends greetings, but with profound esteem, and
with the prayer that for you, now and forever, the day breaks
and the shadows flee away.

Fra Giovanni, A Letter to the Most Illustrious
the Contessina Allagia Dela Aldobrandeschi,
Written Christmas Eve Anno Domini 1513

M-O-T-H-E-R

"M" is for the million things she gave me,
"O" means only that she's growing old,
"T" is for the tears she shed to save me,
"H" is for her heart of purest gold;
"E" is for her eyes, with love-light shining,
"R" means right, and right she'll always be,
Put them all together, they spell "MOTHER,"
A word that means the world to me.

Howard Johnson (c. 1915)

JEANIE WITH THE LIGHT BROWN HAIR

I dream of Jeanie with the light brown hair,
Borne, like a vapor, on the summer air,
I see her tripping where the streams play,
Happy as the daisies that dance on her way.
Many were the wild notes her merry voice would pour
Many were the blithe birds that warbled them o'er
I dream of Jeannie with the light brown hair,
Floating like a vapor on the soft, summer air.

I sigh for Jeannie, but her light form strayed
Far from the fond hearts around her native glade;
Her smiles have vanished and her sweet songs flown,
Flitting like the dreams that have cheered us and gone.
Now the nodding wild flowers may wither on the shore,
While her gentle fingers will cull them no more;
I dream of Jeannie with the light brown hair,
Floating like a vapor on the soft, summer air.

Stephen C. Foster (1826-1864)

TO NELLIE

Whose devotion through the years
Deserves a greater tribute.

Edgar A. Guest (1881-1959)
Tribute of Lifetime Work of Poetry to His Wife

AVE MARIA

Ave Maria! Maiden mild,
Ah! listen to a maiden's prayer;
For thou canst hear, though from the wild,
'Tis Thou, 'tis Thou canst save amid despair.
Safe may we sleep until the morrow,
Though banish'd, outcast and revil'd.
Oh Maiden, see a maiden's sorrow;
Oh Mother, hear—a suppliant child!
Ave Maria!

Ave Maria! Undefil'd!
The flinty couch whereon we're sleeping
Shall seem with down of eider pil'd,
If Thou above sweet watch art keeping.
The murky cavern's air so heavy
Shall breathe of balm if Thou hast smiled;
Then, Maiden, hear a maiden pleading,
Oh Mother, hear—a suppliant child!
Ave Maria!

Ave Maria! Stainless styl'd!
Each fiend of air or earthly essence,
From this their wonted haunt exil'd,
Shall flee before Thy holy presence!
We bow, beneath our cares o'er-laden,
Now to Thy guidance reconcil'd;
Then hear, oh Maiden, a simple maiden,
And for a father hear—a child!
Ave Maria!

Sir Walter Raleigh (1552?-1618)

EVE'S GRAVE

Wheresoever she was, *there* was Eden.

Mark Twain (1835-1910)

BARBARA FRIETCHIE

Up from the meadows rich with corn
Clear in the cool September morn,

The clustered spires of Frederick stand
Green-walled by the hills of Maryland.

Round about them orchards sweep,
Apple and peach tree rooted deep,

Fair as a garden of the Lord,
To the eyes of the famished rebel horde,

On that pleasant morn of the early fall
When Lee marched over the mountain wall—

Over the mountains winding down,
Horse and foot into Frederick town.

Forty flags with silver stars,
Forty flags with their crimson bars,

Flapped in the morning wind; the sun
Of noon looked down, and saw not one.

Up rose old Barbara Frietchie then,
Bowed with her fourscore years and ten;

Bravest of all in Frederick town,
She took up the flag the men hauled down;

In her attic window the staff she set,
To show that one heart was loyal yet.

Up the street came the royal tread,
Stonewall Jackson riding ahead.

Under his slouch hat left and right
He glanced: the old flag met his sight.

"Halt!"—the dust-brown ranks stood fast;
"Fire!"—out blazed the rifle blast.

It shivered the window, pane and sash;
It rent the banner with seam and gash.

Quick, as it fell from the broken staff
Dame Frietchie snatched the silken scarf;

She leaned far out on the window-sill,
And shook it forth with a royal will.

"Shoot if you must this old grey head,
But spare your country's flag," she said.

A shade of sadness, a blush of shame,
Over the face of the leader came;

The nobler nature within him stirred
To life at that woman's deed and word:

"Who touches a hair of yon gray head
Dies like a dog! March on" he said.

All day long through Frederick street
Sounded the tread of marching feet:

All day long that free flag tost
Over the heads of the rebel host.

Ever its torn folds rose and fell
On the loyal winds that loved it well;

And through the hill-gaps sunset light
Shone over it with a warm good-night.

Barbara Frietchie's work is o'er.
And the rebel rides on his raids no more.

Honor to her! and let the tear
Fall, for her sake on Stonewall's bier.

Over Barbara Frietchie's grave,
Flag of freedom and union wave!

Peace and order and beauty draw
Round thy symbol of light and law;

And ever the stars above look down
On thy stars below in Frederick town.

John Greenleaf Whittier (1807-1892)

NORTH STAR

For that which the female does to create, enrich, and pro-
long life, for her gentle, unselfish nature and devotion to the
sick and needy, and her unbridled beneficence to all, should
not this North Star of the species, in a loving, appreciative
and compassionate sense, be exempted from major illness,
physical pain, suffering, plagues and afflictions? Has she not
earned, in consideration of her goodness, benefit, and never
ending personal sacrifice in behalf of others, full and complete reprieve and exemption from life's ills? Would not every
considerate and responsible person agree and confess that
this benevolent, lovely creature is duly entitled to this and
more?

Sidney S. Smith (1928-   )

WONDERFUL MOTHER

God made a wonderful mother,
A mother who never grows old;
He made her smile of the sunshine,
And He moulded her heart of pure gold;
In her eyes He placed bright shining stars,
In her cheeks fair roses you see;
God made a wonderful mother,
And He gave that dear mother to me.

Pat O'Reilly

INNOCENCE

Miranda, was the innocent daughter of Prospero in Shakespeare's *The Tempest*, raised without human companions. She is overcome with awe at the first persons she sees:

O wonder!
How many goodly creatures there are here!
How beauteous mankind is! Oh, brave new world,
That has such people in't!

MARRIAGE

Grow old along with me!
   The best is yet to be.
The last of life, for which the first was made:
   Our times are in His hand
Who saith: "A whole I planned,
   Youth sees but half: trust God, see all,
      nor be afraid."

Robert Browning (1812-1889), from "Rabbi Ben Ezra"

TO MY MOTHER

Because I feel that in the heavens above
    The angels, whispering one to another,
Can find among their burning terms of love,
    None so devotional as that of "Mother,"
Therefore by that dear name I have long called you,
    You who are more than mother unto me,
And fill my heart of hearts, where death installed you,
    In setting my Virginia's spirit free.
My mother—my own mother, who died early,
    Was but the mother of myself; but you
Are the mother to the one I loved so dearly,
    And thus are dearer than the mother I knew
But that infinity with which my wife
Was dearer to my soul than its soul-life.

Edgar Allan Poe (1809-1849)

SUMMUM BONUM

All the breath and the bloom of the year in the bag of one
    bee:
All the wonder and wealth of the mine in the heart of one
    gem:
In the core of one pearl all the shade and the shine of the sea:
Breath and bloom, shade and shine, . . . wonder, wealth,
    and . . . how far above them . . .
        Truth, That's brighter than one gem,
        Trust, that's purer than pearl . . .
Brightest truth, purest trust in the universe . . . all were for
    me
In the kiss of one girl.

Robert Browning (1812-1889)

LOVE

Love is not getting old, but giving, not a wild dream of pleasure, and a madness of desire . . . oh, no, love is not that—it is goodness and honor, and peace and pure living, yes, love is that; and it is the best thing in the world, and the thing that lives longest.

Henry Van Dyke (1852-1933)

WOMAN'S BEAUTY

He feels it in the beauty of a woman—in the grace of her step—in the lustre of her eye—in the melody of her voice—in her self-laughter—in her sigh—in the harmony of the rustling of her robes. He deeply feels it in her winning endearments—in her burning enthusiasm—in her gentle charities—in her meek and devotional endurances, but above all—ah! far above all—he kneels to it—he worships it in the faith—in the purity—in the strength—in the altogether divine majesty of her love.

Edgar Allen Poe (1809-1849)

NATURE OF LOVE

Love is a sour delight, a sugar'd grief,
A living death, and ever dying life;
A breach of reason's law, a secret thief,
A sea of tears, an everlasting strife;
A bait for fools, a scourge of noble wits,
A deadly wound, a shot which ever hits.

Thomas Watson (1557-1592), from the *Passionate Century of Love*

MOTHERHOOD

The bravest battle that ever was fought!
    Shall I tell you where and when?
On the maps of the world you will find it not;
    'Twas fought by the mothers of men.

Nay, not with the cannon of battle-shot,
    With a sword or noble pen;
Nay, not with eloquent words or thought
    From mouths of wonderful men!

But deep in a walled-up woman's heart—
    Of a woman that would not yield,
But bravely, silently bore her part—
    Lo, there is the battlefield!

No marshalling troops, no bivouac song,
    No banner to gleam and wave;
But oh! these battles, they last so long—
    From babyhood to the grave.

Yet, faithful still as a bridge of stars,
    She fights in her walled-up town—
Fights on and on in her endless wars,
    Then silent, unseen, goes down.

Oh, ye with banners and battle-shot,
    And soldiers to shout and praise!
I tell you the kingliest victories fought
    Were fought in those silent ways.

O spotless woman in a world of shame,
With splendid and silent scorn,
Go back to God as white as you came—
The kingliest warrior born!

                     Joaquin Miller (1839-1913)

TRIBUTE

You have been a lifetime of joy to your family, friends, and neighbors.

You have demonstrated and taught the finest qualities of manhood and womanhood.

You have exemplified in your marriage the highest possible concepts of love and unity.

You have stood for principle, integrity, love, kindness, generosity, and goodness.

You have withstood the greatest personal loss of loved ones, and still kept your heads erect.

You have seen with keen eyes the faults and foibles of others without bending in your own beliefs.

You have loved others in such a way that they will in turn never stop loving you.

You have loved your God and inspired others to possess the same unfailing love for the Supreme Creator.

For all of these things and the many others that I have come to know you for, this tribute is offered respectfully and with great love and admiration.

Sidney S. Smith (1928-   )

BROKEN-HEARTED

But to see her was to love her
Love but her, and love forever.
Had we never loved sae kindly,
Had we never loved sae blindly,
Never met—or never parted—
We had ne'er been broken-hearted.

Robert Burns (1759-1796)

HARMONY

I shall define beauty to be a harmony of all the parts in whatsoever subject it appears fitted together with such proportion and connection that nothing could be added, diminished or altered, but for the worse.

Leon Batista Alberti (1240?-1472)

TO HELEN

Helen, thy beauty is to me
   Like those Nicean barks of yore,
That gently o'er a perfumed sea,
   Thy weary, way-worn wanderer bore
   To his native shore.

Our desperate seas long wont to roam,
   Thy hyacinth hair, thy classic face,
Thy Naiad airs have brought me home
   To the glory that was Greece,
      And the grandeur that was Rome.

Lo! in yon brilliant window niche
   How status-like I see thee stand,
The agate lamp within thy hand!
   Ah, Psyche, from the regions which
   Are Holy-Land!

               Edgar Allan Poe (1809-1849)

IN THE SHADE OF THE OLD APPLE TREE

Refrain

In the shade of the old apple tree
Where the love in your eyes I could see,
When the voice that I heard,
Like the song of the birds,
Seem'd to whisper sweet music to me;
I could hear the dull buzz of the bee
In the blossoms as you said to me,
With a heart that was true,
"I'll be waiting for you,
In the shade of the old apple tree."

               Harry H. Williams (1874-1924)

MOTHERS

Because they are co-partners with God in perpetuating life upon earth, they are a cut above others. Their nature, physically and mentally, is specifically designed to propagate the species. In parenting they have more natural love, tenderness, mercy, faith, hope, and charity, more patience, self-discipline, tenacity, and sound judgement, than their counterparts, males.

In the process of procreation, the woman's mind and body are sleek instruments deserving admiration. To both child and man, she is the embodiment of beauty, charm, and intelligence. Her body and mind are well suited for survival. As mother and mate, she is indomitable and resilient. Her instinctual wisdom, wit, and tenacity set her apart to establish and defend home and nursery for mate and brood.

The male of the species marvels at the miracle of womanhood and motherhood, yet never quite fully comprehends and accepts her extraordinary breadth and scope in action. All in all, owing to her unique, complex nature and role in the propagation of the species, an estimated seventy-five billion souls have lived upon this host earth.

Sidney S. Smith (1928-   )

HARK! HARK! THE LARK

Hark! Hark! the lark at heaven's gate sings,
    And Phoebus 'gins arise,
His steeds to water at those springs
    On chaliced flowers that lies;
And winking Mary-buds begin
    To ope their golden eyes.
With everything that pretty is,
    My lady sweet arise;
        Arise! Arise!

William Shakespeare (1564-1616)

LOVE'S OLD SWEET SONG

Once in the dear dead days beyond recall,
When on the world the mists began to fall,
Out of the dreams that rose in happy throng,
Low in our hearts, Love sang an old sweet song;
And in the dusk where fell the firelight gleam,
Softly it wove itself into our dream.

Even today we hear love's song of yore,
Deep in our hearts it dwells forever more.
Footsteps may falter, weary grow the way,
Still we can hear it at the close of day.
So till the end, when life's dim shadows fall,
Love will be found the sweetest song of all.

Refrain:

Just a song at twilight, when the lights are low,
And the flick'ring shadows softly come and go.
Tho' the heart be weary, sad the day and long,
Still to us at twilight comes Love's old song,
Comes Love's old sweet song.

Clifton Bingham

BEAUTIFUL DREAMER

Beautiful dreamer, wake unto me,
   Star-light and dew drops are waiting for thee . . .
Sounds of the rude world heard in the day
   Lull'd by the moon-light have all passed away . . .
Beautiful dreamer, queen of my song,
   List' while I woo thee, with soft melody
Gone are the cares of life's busy throng,
   Beautiful dreamer, awake unto me! . . .
   Beautiful dreamer, awake unto me! . . .

Stephen Foster (1826-1864)

DAWN TO DAWN

To every soul, until death overcomes, each new dawn brings something different. For this person . . . a life star rises, for another it sinks; the ship of fate for one sails smoothly, yet another's ship, anchorless and leaking, lists heavily upon rocky shoals; greatness pursues someone else, loneliness plagues another; fortune attends here, impoverishment, hopelessness, and despair prevail there; love's countenance shines upon this soul, hate and envy glare unto another; good friends the happy lot of one, and betrayal the bane of another; knowledge and learning one man's benison, ignorance and poverty another man's crown; here some valor, there some shame; confidence and determination for one, fear and trepidation for another; love and hate, smiles and tears, good and bad, and the list goes on and on ad infinitum. The endless duel in life perpetuates itself. Every soul, God bless it, each one braving the vicissitudes and uncertainties of life. Courageous people: paragons, stalwarts, teachers, confidants, and benefactors . . . brothers and sisters all. Thank Heaven for each and every one.

Sidney S. Smith (1928-   )

HOME, SWEET HOME

"Mid pleasures and palaces, tho' we may roam;
Be it ever so humble, there's no place like home;
A charm from the skies seems to hallow us there,
Which, seek . . . thru' the world, is ne'er met with elsewhere.
Home! Home! Sweet, Sweet Home! There's no place like
    home!
Oh, there is no place like home.

John Howard Payne (1791-1852)

ANGEL MOTHER

All that I am or ever hope to be, I owe to my angel Mother.

Abraham Lincoln (1809-1865)

TO CELIA

Drink to me only with thine eyes,
　　And I will pledge with mine;
Or leave a kiss but in the cup
　　And I'll not ask for wine.
The thirst that from the soul doth rise
　　Doth ask a drink divine;
But might I of Jove's nectar sup,
　　I would not change for thine.

I send thee late a rosy wreath,
　　Not so much honoring thee
As giving it a hope that there
　　It could not withered be;
But thou thereon dids't only breathe
　　And sent'st back to me;
Since when it grows, and smells, I swear,
　　Not of itself but thee.

Ben Jonson (1573-1637)

MOTHER MACHREE

There's a spot in my heart which no Colleen may own,
There's a depth in my heart never sounded or known:
There's a place in my mem'ry, my life, that you fill,
No other can take it, no one ever will.

Ev'ry sorrow or care in dear days gone by,
Was made bright by the light of the smile in your eye:
Like a candle that's set in the window at night,
Your fond love has cheered me, and guided me right.

Sure, I love the dear silver that shines in your hair,
And the brow that's all furrowed and wrinkled with care.
I kiss the dear fingers, so toil-worn for me,
Oh, God bless you and keep you, Mother Machree!

Ernest R. Ball (1878-1927)

ANNABEL LEE

It was many and many a year ago,
    In a kingdom by the sea,
There lived a maiden whom you may know
    By the name of Annabel Lee;
And this maiden she lived with no other thought
    Than to love and be loved by me.

I was a child and she was a child,
    In this kingdom by the sea:
But we loved with a love that was more than a
love—
    I and my Annabel Lee;
With a love that the winged seraphs of heaven
    Coveted her and me.

And this was the reason that, long ago
    In this kingdom by the sea,
A wind blew out of a cloud, chilling
    My beautiful Annabel Lee;
So that her high-born kinsmen came
    And bore her away from me,
And shut her up in a sepulchre
    In this kingdom by the sea. . . .

But our love it was stronger by far than the love
    Of those who were older than we—
    Of those far wiser than we—
But neither the angels in heaven above,
    Nor the demons down under the sea,
Can ever dissever my soul from the soul
    Of the beautiful Annabel Lee.

For the moon never beams, without bringing me
dreams

Of the beautiful Annabel Lee;
And the stars never rise, but I feel the bright eyes
    Of the beautiful Annabel Lee;
And so all the night-tide, I lie down by the side
Of my darling—my darling—my life and my bride,
    In the sepulchre there by the sea,
    In her tomb by the side of the sea.

Edgar Allan Poe (1809-1849)

THE LIVING JULIET

He jests at scars that never felt a wound. . . .
But, soft! what light through yonder window breaks?
It is the east, and Juliet is the sun!
Arise, fair sun, and kill the envious moon,
Who is already sick and pale with grief,
That thou her maid art far more fair than she.
Be not her maid, since she is envious;
Her vestal livery is but sick and green,
And none but fools do wear it; cast it off.
It is my lady; O, it is my love!
O, that she knew she were!
She speaks, yet she says nothing. What of that?
Her eye discourses, I will answer it.
I am too bold, 'tis not to me she speaks:
Two of the fairest stars in all the heaven,
Having some business, do entreat her eyes
To twinkle in their spheres till they return.
What if her eyes were there, they in her head?
The brightness of her cheek would shame those stars,
As daylight doth a lamp; her eyes in heaven
Would through the airy region stream so bright
That birds would sing and think it were not night.

William Shakespeare (1564-1616), from Romeo and Juliet

TOUCH OF LOVE

The fountains mingle with the river,
    And the rivers with the ocean,
The winds of heaven mix forever
    With a sweet emotion;
Nothing in the world is single;
    All things by a law divine
In one another's being mingle;
    Why not I with thine?

See the mountains kiss high heaven,
    And the waves clasp one another;
No sister flower would be forgiven
    If it disdained its brother;
And the sunlight clasps the earth,
    And the moonbeams kiss the sea;
What are these kissings worth,
    If thou kiss not me?

Percy Bysshe Shelley (1792-1822)

NIGHTFALL

I need so much the quiet of your love
After the day's loud strife;
I need your calm all other things above
After the stress of life.

I crave the haven that in your dear heart lies,
After all toil is done;
I need the starshine of your heavenly eyes,
After the day's great sun.

Charles Hanson Towne (1877-1949)

PHANTOM OF DELIGHT

She was a phantom of delight
When first she gleamed upon my sight;
A lovely apparition sent
To be moment's ornament;
Her eyes as stars of twilight fair;
Like twilight's, too, her dusky hair;
But all things else about her drawn
From May-time and the cheerful dawn;
A dancing shape, an image gay,
To haunt, to startle, and waylay.

I saw her upon nearer view,
A Spirit, yet a Woman too!
Her household motions light and free,
And steps of virgin liberty;
A countenance in which did meet
Sweet records, promises as sweet;
A creature not too bright or good
For human nature's daily food;
For transient sorrows, simple wiles,
Praise, blame, love, kisses, tears, and smiles.

And now I see with eye serene
The very pulse of the machine
A being breathing thoughtful breath,
A traveller between life and death;
The reason firm, the temperate will,
Endurance, foresight, strength, and skill;
A perfect woman nobly plann'd,
To warm, to comfort, and command;
And yet a spirit still, and bright
With something of angelic light.

William Wordsworth (1770-1850)

SHE WALKS IN BEAUTY

She walks in beauty like the night
Of cloudless climes and starry skies,
And all that's best of dark and bright
Meet in her aspect and her eyes;
Thus mellowed to that tender light
Which heaven to gaudy day denies.

One shade the more, one ray the less,
Had half impaired the nameless grace
Which waves in every raven tress
Or softly lightens o'er the face,
Where thoughts serenely sweet express
How pure, how dear their dwelling place.

And on the cheek, and o'er that brow,
So soft, so calm, yet eloquent,
The smiles that win, the tints that glow
But tell of days in goodness spent,
A mind at peace with all below,
A heart whose love is innocent.

Lord Byron (1788-1824)

KNOWN WRONG

The study of history is useful to the
historian by teaching him his ignorance
of women. . . . The woman who is known only
through a man is known wrong.

Henry Brooks Adams (1838-1918)

Every physical quality admired by men in women is in direct
connection with the manifold functions of the woman for
the propagation of the species.

James Joyce (1882-1941)

MAUD MULLER

Maud Muller, on a summer's day,
Raked the meadow sweet with hay.
Beneath her torn hat glowed the wealth
Of simple beauty and rustic health.
Singing she wrought, and her merry glee
The mock-bird echoed from the tree.

But when she glanced at the far-off town,
White from its hill-slope looking down,
The sweet song died and a vague unrest
And a nameless longing filled her breast;
A wish, that she hardly dared to own,
For something better than she had known.

The Judge rode slowly down the lane,
Stroking his horse's chestnut mane:
He drew his bridle in the shade
Of an apple tree to greet the maid,
And asked a drink from a spring that flowed
Through the meadow and across the road.

She stooped where the clear stream bubbled up,
And filled for him her small tin cup,
And blushed as she gave it looking down
On her feet so bare, and her tattered gown.
"Thanks!" said the Judge, "a sweeter draught
From a fairer hand was never quaffed."

He spoke of the grass, and flowers, and trees,
Of the singing birds and the humming bees;
Then talked of the haying, and wondered whether
The clouds in the west would bring foul weather.
And Maud forgot her briar-torn gown,
And her graceful ankles so bare and brown,
And listened, while a pleased surprise
Looked from her long-lashed hazel eyes.

At last as one who for delay
Seeks a vain excuse, he rode away.
Maud Muller looked and sighed: "Ah, me!
That I the judge's bride might be!
He would dress me up in silks so fine,
And praise and toast me at his wine.

"My father should wear a broadcloth coat;
My brother should sail a painted boat;
I'd dress my mother so grand and gay,
And the baby should have a new toy each day;
And I'd feed the hungry and clothe the poor,
And all should bless me who left our door."

The Judge looked down as he climbed the hill,
And saw Maud Muller standing still.
"A form more fair, a face more sweet,
Ne'er has it been my lot to meet;
And her modest answer and graceful air
Show her wise and good as she is fair.

"Would she were mine, and I to-day,
Like her, a harvester of hay:
No doubtful balance of rights and wrongs,
No weary lawyers with endless tongues;
But low of cattle and song of birds,
And health, and quiet, and loving words."

But he thought of his sisters proud and cold,
And his mother, vain of her rank and gold;
So, closing his heart, the Judge rode on,
And Maud was left in the field alone.
But the lawyers smiled that afternoon,
When he hummed in court an old love-tune;
And the young girl mused beside the well,
Till the rain on the unraked clover fell.

He wedded a wife of richest dower,
Who lived for fashion, as he for power;
Yet oft, in his marble hearth's bright glow,
He watched a picture come and go;
And sweet Maud Muller's hazel eyes,
Looked out in their innocent surprise.

Oft when the wine in his glass was red,
He longed for the wayside well instead;
And closed his eyes on his garnished rooms,
To dream of meadows and clover-blooms.
And the proud man sighed, with a secret pain,
"Ah, that I were free again!
Free as when I rode that day,
Where the barefoot maiden raked her hay."

She wedded a man unlearned and poor,
And many children played round her door;
But care and sorrow and wasting pain
Left their traces on heart and brain.
And oft when the summer sun shone hot
On the new-mown hay in the meadow lot,
And she heard the little spring brook fall
Over the roadside, through the wall,
In the shade of the apple-tree again
She saw a rider draw his rein,
And gazing down with timid grace,
She felt his pleased eyes read her face.

Sometimes her narrow kitchen walls
Stretched away into stately halls;
The weary wheel a spinet turned:
The tallow candle an astral burned;
And for him who sat by the chimney lug,
Dozing and grumbling o'er pipe and mug,
A manly form at her side she saw

And joy was duty and love was law.
Then she took up her burden of life again.
Saying only, "It might have been!"

Alas for maiden, alas for Judge,
For rich repiner and household drudge!
God pity them both! and pity us all,
Who vainly the dreams of youth recall;
For of all sad words of tongue and pen
The saddest are these: "It might have been!"
Ah, well! for us all some sweet hope lies
Deeply buried from human eyes;
And in the hereafter angels may
Roll the stone from its grave away!

John Greenleaf Whittier (1807-1892)

SONNET 18

Shall I compare thee to a summer's day?
Thou art more lovely and more temperate:
Rough winds do shake the darling buds of May
And summer's lease hath all too short a date:
Sometimes too hot the eye of heaven shines,
And often is his gold complexion dimm'd
And every fair from fair sometimes declines
By chance, or nature's changing course, untrimmed.
But the eternal summer shall not fade
Nor lose possession of that fair thou ownest;
Nor shall Death brag thou wanderest in his shade,
When in eternal lines to time thou growest:
So long as men can breathe, or eyes can see
So long lives this, and this gives life to thee.

William Shakespeare (1564-1616)

Every woman is the gift of a world to me.

Heinrich Heine from *Ideas: The Book Le Grand* (1797-1856)

TO ANTHEA,
WHO MAY COMMAND HIM ANYTHING

Bid me to live, and I will live
   Thy protestant to be:
Or bid me love, and I will give
   A loving heart to thee.

A heart as soft, a heart as kind,
   A heart as sound and free
As in the whole world thou canst find,
   That heart I'll give to thee.

Bid that heart stay, and it will stay,
   To honor thy decree:
Or bid it languish quite away,
   And it shall do so for thee.

Bid me to weep, and I will weep
   When I have eyes to see:
And having none, yet I will keep
   A heart to weep for thee.

Bid me despair, and I'll despair,
   Under that cypress tree:
Or bid me die, and I will dare
   E'en Death, to die for thee.

Thou art my life, my love, my heart,
   The very eyes of me,
And hast command of every part,
   To live and die for thee.

Robert Herrick (1591-1674)

SHE DWELT AMONG THE UNTRODDEN WAYS

She dwelt among the untrodden ways
   Besides the springs of Dove,
A maid whom there were none to praise
   And very few to love:

A violet by a mossy stone
   Half hidden from the eye.
Fair as a star, when only one
   Is shining in the sky.

She lived unknown, and few could know
   When Lucy ceased to be;
But she is in her grave, and, oh,
   The difference to me.

William Wordsworth (1770-1850)

FATE

For it is the fate of a woman
Long to be patient and silent, to wait like a ghost
   that is speechless,
Till some questioning voice dissolves the spell of
   its silence.
Hence is the inner life of so many suffering
   women
Sunless and silent and deep, like subterranean
   rivers
Running through caverns of darkness, unheard,
   unseen, and unfruitful,
Chafing their channels of stone, with endless and
   profitless murmurs.

Henry Wadsworth Longfellow (1807-1882),
from The Courtship of Miles Standish

GOD SAVE THE QUEEN

God save our gracious queen!
Long live our noble queen!
God save the queen!
Send her victorious,
Happy and glorious,
Long to reign over us;
God save the queen!

Thy choicest gifts in store
On her be pleased to pour;
Long may she reign!
May she defend our laws,
And ever give us cause
To sing with heart and voice,
God save the queen!

Unknown

ON HIS DECEASED WIFE

Methought I saw my late espoused Saint
Brought to me like Alcestis from the grave,
Whom Jove's great Son to her glad Husband gave,
Rescued from death by force though pale and faint.
Mine as whom washed from spot of child-bed taint,
Purification in the old Law did save,
And such, as yet once more I trust to have
Full sight of her in Heaven without restraint,
Came vested all in white, pure as her mind:
Her face was veiled, yet to my fancied sight,
Love, sweetness, goodness, in her person shined
So clear, as in no face with more delight.
But O as to embrace me she inclined
I waked, she fled, and day brought back my night.

John Milton (1608-1674)

THAT WONDERFUL MOTHER OF MINE

The moon never beams without bringing me dreams
Of that wonderful mother of mine.
The birds never sing but a message they bring
Of that wonderful mother of mine.
Just to bring back the time, that was so sweet to me,
Just to bring back the days, when I sat on her knee.

I pray ev'ry night to our Father above,
For that wonderful mother of mine.
I ask Him to keep her as long as He can
That—wonderful mother of mine.
There are treasures on earth, that made life seem
        worthwhile,
But there's none can compare to my dear mother's smile.

Refrain

You are a wonderful mother, dear old Mother of mine.
You'll hold a spot down deep in my heart,
'Till the stars no longer shine.
Your soul shall live on forever,
On through the fields of time.
For there'll never be another to me,
Like that wonderful Mother of mine.

                                              Clyde Hager

WHEN WE TWO PARTED

When we two parted
    In silence and tears,
Half broken-hearted
    To sever for years,

Pale grew thy cheek and cold,
    Colder thy kiss;
Truly that hour foretold
    Sorrow to this.

The dew of the morning
    Sunk chill on my brow—
It felt like the warning
    Of what I feel now.
Thy vows are all broken,
    And light is thy fame;
I hear thy name spoken,
    And share in its shame.

They name thee before me,
    A knell to mine ear;
A shudder comes o'er me—
    Why wert thou so dear?
They know not I knew thee,
    Who knew thee too well:—
Long, long shall I rue thee,
    Too deeply to tell.

In secret we met—
    In silence I grieve
That thy heart could forget,
    Thy spirit deceive.
If I should meet thee
    After long years,
How should I greet thee?—
    With silence and tears.

Lord Byron (1788-1824)

We have seen an American woman write a novel which
. . . was read with equal interest to three audiences, namely,
in the parlor, in the kitchen, and in the nursery of every
house.

Ralph Waldo Emerson (1803-1882)

A RED, RED ROSE

O my Luv's like a red, red rose
    That's newly sprung in June:
O my Luv's like the melodie
    That's sweetly played in tune!

As fair art thou, my bonnie lass,
    So deep in luv am I:
And I will luv thee still, my dear,
    Till a' the seas gang dry:

Till a' the seas gang dry, my dear,
    And the rocks melt wi' the sun;
I will luv thee still, my dear,
    While the sands o' life shall run.

And fare thee weel, my only Luv,
    And fare thee weel a while!
And I will come again, my Luv,
    Tho' it were ten thousand mile.

                                    Robert Burns (1759-1796)

Her heart was the abode of heavenly purity. She had no feelings but of kindness and beneficience. ... She had known sorrow, but her sorrow was silent. . . . if there is existence and retribution beyond the grave, my mother is happy.

                                    John Quincy Adams (1767-1848)

You see that boy of mine? Though but five, he governs the universe. Yes, for he rules his mother, his mother rules me, I rule Athens, and Athens the world.

                                    Themistocles (52?-460 B.C.)

THE BALLAD OF DEAD LADIES OF FRANCOIS VILLON

Tell me now in what hidden way is
    Lady Flora the lovely Roman?
Where's Hipparchia, and where is Thais,
    Neither of them the fairer woman?
    Where is Echo, beheld of no man,
Only heard on river and mere, —
    She whose beauty was more than human? . . .
But where are the snows of yesteryear?

Where's Heloise, the learned nun,
    For whose sake Abeillard, I ween,
Lost manhood and put priesthood on?
    (From Love he won such dule and teen!)
    And where, I pray you, is the Queen
Who willed that Buridan should steer
    Sewed in a sack's mouth down the Seine? . . .
But where are the snows of yesteryear?

White Queen Blanche, like a queen of lilies,
    With a voice like any mermaiden, —
Bertha Broadfoot, Beatrice, Alice,
    And Ermengarde the lady of Maine, —
    And that good Joan whom Englishmen
At Rouen doomed and burned her there, —
    Mother of God, where are they then? . . .
But where are the snows of yester-year?

Nay, never ask this week, fair lord,
    Where they are gone, nor yet this year,
Save with this much for an overword, —
    But where are the snows of yesteryear?

Dante Gabriel Rossetti (1828-1882)

WHO IS SYLVIA

Who is Sylvia? What is she,
    That all our swains commend her?
Holy, fair, and wise is she;
    The heaven's did such grace lend her,
That she might admired be.

Is she kind as she is fair?
    For beauty lives with kindness.
Love doth to her eyes repair,
    To help him out of his blindness;
And, being helped, inhabits there.

Then to Sylvia let us sing,
    That Sylvia is excelling;
She excels each mortal thing,
    Upon the dull earth dwelling:
To her let us garlands bring.

William Shakespeare (1564-1616),
from *Two Gentlemen of Verona*

EVE'S DIARY

It is my prayer, it is my longing, that we may pass from this life together—a longing which shall never perish from the earth, but shall have place in the heart of every wife that loves, until the end of time; and it shall be called by my name.

But if one of us must go first, it is my prayer that it shall be I; for he is strong, I am weak, I am not so necessary to him as he is to me—life without him would not be life; how could I endure it? This prayer is also immortal, and will not cease from being offered up while my race continues. I am the first wife; and in the last wife I shall be repeated.

Mark Twain (1835-1910)

SILVER THREADS AMONG THE GOLD

Darling I am growing old,
Silver threads among the gold,
Shine upon my brow today;
Life is fading fast away.
But my darling you will be, will be,
Always young and fair to me.
Yes my darling you will be,
Always young and fair to me.

Darling I am growing, growing old,
Silver threads among the gold,
Shine upon my brow today;
Life is fading fast away fast away.

When your hair is silver white
And your cheeks no longer bright,
With the roses of the May
I will kiss your lips and say,
Oh! my darling mine alone, alone,
You have never older grown;
Yes my darling mine alone,
You have never older grown.

Darling I am growing, growing old,
Silver threads among the gold,
Shine upon my brow today;
Life is fading fast away fast away.

Love can never more grow old,
Locks may lose their brown and gold;
Cheeks may fade and hollow grow
But the hearts that love will know.
Never, never winter's frost and chill,
Summer's warmth is in them still.
Never winter's frost and chill,
Summer's warmth in them still.

Darling I am growing, growing old,
Silver threads among the gold,
Shine upon my brow today;
Life is fading fast away fast away.

Love is always young and fair
What to us is silver hair?
Faded cheeks or steps grown slow,
To the hearts that beat below.
Since I kissed you mine alone, alone,
You have never older grown.
Since I kissed you mine alone,
You have never older grown.

Darling I am growing, growing old,
Silver threads among the gold,
Shine upon my brow today;
Life is fading fast away fast away.

Alfred M. Durham

DRINK TO ME

Drink to me only with thine eyes, and I will pledge
    with mine,
Or leave a kiss within the cup and I'll not ask for wine;
The thirst that from the soul doth rise, doth ask a
    drink divine,
But might I of Jove's nectar sip, I would not change
    for thine.

I sent thee late a rosy wreath, not so much hon'ring thee,
As giving it a hope that there it could not withered be;
But thou there on did'st only breathe, and send'st it
    back to me,
Since when it grows and smells I swear not of itself, but thee.

Ben Jonson

WHEN YOU AND I WERE YOUNG

I wander'd today to the hill, Maggie,
To watch the scene below,
The creek and the creaking old mill, Maggie,
As we used to long ago.
The green grass is gone from the hill, Maggie,
Where first the daisies sprung;
The creaking old mill is still, Maggie,
Since you and I were young.

A city so silent and lone, Maggie,
Where the young and the gay and the best,
In polished white mansions of stone, Maggie,
Have each found a place of rest.
Is built where the birds used to play, Maggie,
And join in the songs that were sung;
For we sang as gay as they, Maggie,
When you and I were young.

They say I am feeble with age, Maggie,
My steps are less sprightly than then,
My face is a well written page, Maggie,
But time alone was the pen.
They say we are aged and gray, Maggie,
As sprays by the white breaker's flung;
But to me you're as fair as you were, Maggie,
When you and I were young.

George W. Johnson

Give me a look, give me a face,
That makes simplicity a grace;
Robes loosely flowing, hair as free, —
Such sweet neglect more taketh me
Than all the adulteries of art;
They strike mine eyes, but not my heart.

Ben Jonson (1573-1637)

MOTHER AND CHILD

The wind blew wide the casement, and within—
It was the loveliest picture!—a sweet child
Lay in its mother's arms, and drew its life,
In pauses, from the fountain,—the white round
Part shaded by loose tresses, soft and dark,
Concealing, but still showing, the fair realm
Of so much rapture, as green shadowing trees
With beauty shroud the brooklet. The red lips
Were parted, and the cheek upon the breast
Lay close, and, like the young leaf of the flower,
Wore the same color, rich and warm and fresh:—
And such alone are beautiful. Its eye,
A full blue gem, most exquisitely set,
Looked archly on its world,—the little imp,
As if it knew even then that such a wreath
Were not for all; and with its playful hands
It drew aside the robe that hid its realm,
And peeped and laughed aloud, and so it laid
Its head upon the shrine of such pure joys,
And, laughing, slept. And while it slept, the tears
Of the sweet mother fell upon its cheek,—
Tears such as fall from April skies, and bring
The sunlight after. They were tears of joy;
And the true heart of that young mother then
Grew lighter, and she sang unconsciously
The silliest ballad-song that ever yet
Subdued the nursery's voices, and brought sleep
To fold her sabbath wings above its couch.

William Gilmore Simms (1806-1870)

For a better and a higher gift than this there cannot be, when with accordant aims man and wife have a home. Great grief is it to foes and joy to friends; but they themselves best know its meaning.

Homer (circa 850 B.C.)
Odyssey, Book VI, Line 182

6

LANGUAGE OF MARRIAGE

The Crown of the house is Godliness
The Beauty of the house is Order.
The Glory of the house is Hospitality.
The Blessing of the house is Contentment.

Old Inscription

ONE FLESH

For this cause shall a man leave his father and mother, and cleave to his wife; And they twain shall be one flesh: . . . What therefore God hath joined together, let not man put asunder.

New Testament, Mark 10:6-9

RICHER THAN GOLD

You may have tangible wealth untold;
Caskets of jewels and coffers of gold.
Richer than I you can never be—
I had a mother who read to me.

Strickland Gillilian

The trouble with being a parent is that by the time you are experienced you are usually unemployed.

Author Unknown

MOTHER'S SONGS

Songs my mother taught me,
In the days long vanish'd
Seldom from her eyelids
Were the teardrops banish'd.
Now I teach my children
Each melodious measure,
Oft the teardrops flowing,
Oft they flow from my mem'ry's treasure.

Author Unknown

BIRTHSTONES

Feminine	Masculine
January—Garnet	January—Gold Seal Ring
February—Amethyst	February—Cat's Eye
March—Aquamarine	March—Bloodstone
April—Diamond	April—Diamond
May—Emerald	May—Gold Seal Ring
June—Pearl	June—Agate Seal Ring
July—Ruby	July—Onyx
August—Sardonyx	August—Carnelian
September—Sapphire	September—Sapphire
October—Opal	October—Opal
November—Topaz	November—Topaz
December—Turquoise or Lapis Lazuli	December—Gold Seal Ring

WEDDING ANNIVERSARIES

1 Year — Paper
5 Years — Wood
10 Years — Tin, Aluminum
15 Years — Crystal
20 Years — China
25 Years — Silver
50 Years — Gold
60 Years — Diamond

"Something old, something new,
Something borrowed, something blue,
And a lucky sixpence in your shoe?"

PITY AND FORGIVE

The kindest and the happiest pair,
   Will find occasion to forbear;
Find something every day they live,
   To pity, and perhaps forgive.

William Cowper (1731-1800)

QUEEN

I would have them desire and claim the title of Lady, provided they claim, not merely the title, but the office and duty signified by it. . . . Queens you must always be; . . . queens to your husbands and your sons; queens . . . to the world beyond, which bows itself . . . [to] the stainless scepter of womanhood.

John Ruskin (1819-1900)

INDEBTED

The sum which two married people
   owe to one another defies calculation.
It is an infinite debt, which can only
   be discharged through all eternity.

Johann Wolfgang von Goethe (1749-1832)

I have spread my dreams under your feet;
Tread softly because you tread on my dreams.

William Butler Yeats (1865-1939)

PILGRIM MARRIAGE

Forth from the curtain of clouds, from
    the tent of purple and scarlet,
Issued the sun, the great High-Priest, in
    his garments resplendent,
Holiness unto the Lord, in letters of light,
    on his forehead,
Round the hem of his robe the golden bells
    and pomegranates.
Blessing the world he came, and the bars
    of vapor beneath him
Gleamed like a grate of brass, and the sea
    at his feet was a laver!
This was the wedding morn of Priscilla
    the Puritan maiden.
Friends were assembled together; the
    Elder and Magistrate also
Graced the scene with their presence, and
    stood like the Law and the Gospel,
One with the sanction of earth and one with
    the blessing of heaven.
Simple and brief was the wedding, as that
    of Ruth and of Boaz,
Softly the youth and the maiden repeated
    the words of betrothal,
Taking each other for husband and wife in
    the Magistrate's presence,
After the Puritan way, and the laudable
    custom of Holland.
Fervently then, and devoutly, the excellent
    Elder of Plymouth
Prayed for the hearth and the home, that
    were founded that day in affection,
Speaking of life and of death, and imploring
    Divine benedictions.

Henry Wadsworth Longfellow (1807-1881),
from the Cocurtship of Miles Standish

LOVE AT HOME

There is beauty all around
    When there's love at home;
There is joy in every sound
    When there's love at home.
Peace and plenty here abide,
Smiling sweet on every side.
Time doth softly, sweetly glide
    When there's love at home.

In the cottage there is joy
    When there's love at home;
Hate and envy ne'er annoy
    When there's love at home.
Roses bloom beneath our feet;
All the earth's a garden sweet,
Making life a bliss complete
    When there's love at home.

Kindly heaven smiles above
    When there's love at home;
All the world is filled with love
    When there's love at home.
Sweeter sings the booklet by;
Brighter beams the azure sky;
Oh, there's One who smiles on high
    When there's love at home.

John Hugh McNaughton (1829-1891)

The most important thing a father can do for his children
is to love their mother.

Author Unknown

HOME

Out of the darkness,
Into its cheeriness,
Come we in weariness
Home

Stephen Chalmers

SUPERIORITY

We are foolish, and without excuse foolish, in speaking of the 'superiority' of one sex to the other, as if they could be compared. . . . Each completes the other, and is completed by the other. . . . You may chisel a boy into shape, as you would a rock, or hammer him into it, if he be of a better kind, as you would a piece of bronze. But you cannot hammer a girl into anything. She grows as a flower does . . . you cannot fetter her; she must take her own fair form and way, and have — "Her household motions light and free, And steps of virgin liberty."

John Ruskin (1819-1900)

FAMILY GOVERNMENT

There is little less trouble in governing a private family than a whole kingdom.

Michel E. Montaigne (1533-1592)

A truly happy marriage is one in which a woman gives the best years of her life to the man who made them the best.

Author Unknown

TRIFLES

A great proportion of the wretchedness which has embit-
tered married life, has originated in a negligence of trifles. . . .
It is a sensitive plant, which will not bear even the touch of
unkindness; a delicate flower, which indifference will chill
and suspicion blast. It must be watered by the showers of
tender affection, expanded by the cheering glow of kindness,
and guarded by the impregnable barrier of unshaken confidence. Thus matured, it will bloom with fragrance in every
season of life, and sweeten even the loneliness of declining
years.

Thomas Sprat (1635-1713)

ORDER OF THE HOME

The education of a child begins in infancy. At six months
old it can answer smile by smile, and impatience with impatience. It can observe, enjoy, and suffer. Do you suppose it
makes no difference to it that the order of the house is perfect
and quiet, the faces of its father and mother full of peace,
their soft voices familiar to its ear, and even those of stran-
gers, loving; or that it is tossed from arm to arm, [in a] . . .
reckless . . . household, or in the confusion of a gay one? The
moral dispostion is, I doubt not, greatly determined in those
first speechless years.

John Ruskin (1819-1900)

RESTLESSNESS

The best cure for restlessness for far places is to go there
and find them full of people who would like to get back home
again.

Anne Sophie Swetchine (1782-1857)

CONNECTION

He that has . . . no such connecting interests . . . as a home and a family . . . is exposed to temptation, to idleness, and in danger of becoming useless, if not a burden and a nuisance in society.

Samuel Johnson (1709-1784)

WONDERFUL MARRIAGE

One of my students wrote me announcing his engagement. "This is not going to be much of a wedding," he said, "but it is going to be a wonderful marriage."

William Lyon Phelps (1865-1943)

GREATNESS

So much of what is great . . . has sprung from the closeness of the family ties.

Sir James M. Barrie (1860-1937)

An ideal wife is any woman who has an ideal husband.

Booth Tarkington (1869-1946)

ADVENTURE

With death, marriage is one of life's two greatest adventures. . . . I would keep it an adventure — an adventure in happiness.

Frances Starr

INFANCY

Would you have your son obedient to you when past a child; be sure then to . . . imprint it in his infancy; . . . so shall you have him . . . obedient . . . whilst he is a child, and your affectionate friend when he is a man. . . . For the time must come, when [he] will be past the rod and correction; . . . and he that is a good, a virtuous, and able man, must be made so within. And therefore what he is to receive from education, what is to sway and influence his life, must be something . . . woven into the very principles of his nature . . . The little, or almost insensible impressions on our tender infancies, have very important and lasting consequences.

John Locke (1632-1704)

I think we are inclined to forget that youth and beauty are [after] all . . . only lures. They are not binders . . . We stress too much the externals and forget too much the realities . . . There are greater hazaards to marriage than attraction for other people.

Margaret W. Jackson

LESSONS

"The home is the source of our national life," said David O. McKay. It is also the source of our personal lives, and in a sense the determiner of our everlasting lives. And so our plea is for parents to take the time it takes to draw near to the children God has given them. Let there be love at home. Let there be tenderness and teaching and caring for and not a shifting of responsibility onto others. God grant that we may never be too busy to do the things that matter most, for "Home makes the man!"

Richard L. Evans (1906-1971)

HOME - HOME

Peace and rest at length have come,
  All the day's long toil is past;
And each heart is whispering, 'Home,
  Home at last!'

Thomas Hood (1799-1845)

MANNERS

It is a common saying that "Manners make the man;" and there is a second, that "Mind makes the man;" but truer than either is a third, that "Home makes the man." For the home-training includes not only manners and mind, but character. It is mainly in the home that the heart is opened, the habits are formed, the intellect is awakened, and character is molded for good or for evil.

Samuel Smiles (1812-1904)

PEACE

He is the happiest, be he king or peasant, who finds peace in his home.

Johann Wolfgang von Goethe (1749-1832)

DUTY

If thou wouldst be happy and easie in thy Family, above all things observe Discipline. Every one in it should know their Duty. . . . And whatever else is done or omitted, be sure to begin and end with God.

William Penn (1644-1718)

TOILING

The home where happiness securely dwells
Was never wrought by charms or magic spells
A mother made it beautiful, but knew
No magic save what toiling hands can do.

Arthur Wallace Peach

HAPPINESS

The happiest moments of my life have been the few which
I have passed at home in the bosom of my family.

Thomas Jefferson (1743-1826)

INTENTION

Whatever woman may cast her lot with mine, should any
ever do so, it is my intention to do all in my power to make
her happy and contented; and there is nothing I can imagine
that would make me more unhappy than to fail in the effort.

Abraham Lincoln (1809-1865)

They shall also teach their children to pray, and to walk
uprightly before the Lord.

Doctrine & Covenants 68:28

Fathers, provoke not your children to wrath; but bring
them up in the nurture and admonition of the Lord.

Ephesians 6:4

A child learns more by imitation than in any other way. Don't we all? And the persons he imitates most blindly and trustingly are bound to be his parents. . . . Nature has made the relationship between parent and child such that beside it any other training bears a certain artificiality.

George Sanderlin

NATURE OF HOME

This is the true nature of home—it is the place of Peace; the shelter, not only from all injury, but from all terror, doubt, and division.

John Ruskin (1819-1900)

BOND

Two persons who have chosen each other out of all the [rest], with the design to be each other's mutual comfort and entertainment, have, in that action, bound themselves to be good-humored, affable, discreet, forgiving, patient, and joyful, with respect to each other's frailties and perfections, to the end of their lives.

Joseph Addison (1672-1719)

PEDIGREE

Man scans with scrupulous care the character and pedigree of his horses, cattle and dogs before he matches them: but when he comes to his own marriage he rarely, or never, takes any such care.

Charles Darwin (1809-1882)

The deepest tenderness a woman can show to a man is to help him do his duty.

Dinah Maria Mulock Craik (1826-1887)

MARRIAGE

Marriage should be something worked toward with every step you take. It shouldn't be an unforeseen emergency, like being called upon unexpectedly to make a speech on a subject you've never heard of.

Margaret Lee Runbeck

I desire no future that will break the ties of the past.

George Eliot (1819-1880)

MOTHER'S PRAYER

I remember my mother's prayers and they have always followed me. They have clung to me all my life.

Abraham Lincoln (1809-1865)

WHERE'S MOTHER?

"Where's Mother," could be heard through the hallway. And they stood and watched her as she went on alone, and the gates closed after her. And they said: "We cannot see her, but she is with us still. A mother like ours is more than a memory. She is a Living Presence."

Temple Bailey (-1953)

It is not good that man should be alone.

Old Testament, Genesis 2:18

SWEET SOUNDS

The sweetest sounds to mortals given
Are heard in Mother, Home and Heaven.

William Goldsmith Brown

Children, obey your parents in all things: for this is well
pleasing unto the Lord.

New Testament, Colossians 3:20

To bear, to nurse, to rear,
To watch and then to lose,
To see my bright ones disappear,
Drawn up like morning dews.

Jean Ingelow

Courage, and be true to one another!

Thomas Carlyle (1795-1881)

Keep thy eyes wide open before marriage; and half shut
afterward.

Thomas Fuller (1608-1661)

Marriage requires the giving and keeping of confidences, the sharing of thoughts and feelings, unfailing respect and understanding, and a frank and gentle communication.

Richard L. Evans

MORAL

It seems that life is all a void,
On selfish thoughts alone employed;
That length of days is not a good,
Unless their use be understood.

Jane Taylor (1783-1824)

Faith that withstood the shocks of toil and time;
    Hope that defied despair;
    Patience that conquered care;
And loyalty, whose courage was sublime;
The great deep heart that was a home for all,—
    Just, eloquent, and strong
    In protest against wrong;
Wide charity, that knew no sin, no fall;
The Spartan spirit that made life so grand,
    Mating poor daily needs
    With high, heroic deeds,
That wrested happiness from Fate's hard hands.

Louisa May Alcott (1832-1888)

GIFT

What gift has Providence bestowed on man that is so dear to him as his children?

Cicero (106-43 B.C.)

The most important work you will do for the Church will be within the walls of your own home.

Harold B. Lee (1899-1973)

Not my will, nor even thy will; but *our* will, subject always to His will.

Author Unknown

TRAVELERS

Children are travelers newly arrived in a strange country of which they know nothing.

John Locke (1632-1704)

COMRADESHIP

Companioned years have made them comprehend
The comradeship that lies beyond a kiss.
The young ask much of life—they ask but this,
To fare the road together to its end.

Roselle Mercier Montgomery

MALE AND FEMALE

Neither is the man without the woman, neither the woman without the man, in the Lord.

New Testament, I Corinthians 11:11

If ever two were one, then surely we.
If ever man were loved by wife, then thee;
If ever wife was happy in a man,
Compare with me ye women if you can.

Anne Bradstreet (1612-1672)

It is not marriage that fails, it is people that fail. All that marriage does is to show people up.

Harry Emerson Fosdick (1878-1969)

'Tis sweet to know there is an eye will mark our coming, and look brighter when we come.

Lord Byron (1788-1824)

The idea that we can leave entirely to children the vital choices of life is unsafe. Leaving such decisions to trial and error is unsafe.

Richard L. Evans (1906-1971)

Train up a child in the way he should go: and when he is old, he will not depart from it.

Old Testament, Proberbs 22:6

IN MEMORY OF A MOTHER

I remember thee in this solemn hour, my dear mother. I remember the days when thou didst dwell on earth, and thy tender love watched over me like a guardian angel. Thou has gone from me, but the bond which unites our souls can never be severed; thine image lives within my heart. May the merciful Father reward thee for the faithfulness and kindness thou hast ever shown me may He lift up the light of His countenance upon thee, and grant thee eternal peace! Amen.

Unknown

HUMBLE BIRTH

And it came to pass in those days, that there went out a decree from Caesar Augustus, that all the world should be taxed.

And all went to be taxed, every one into his own city.

And Joseph also went up from Galilee, out of the city of Nazareth, into Judea, unto the city of David, which is called Bethlehem (because he was of the house and lineage of David:)

To be taxed with Mary his espoused wife, being great with child.

And she brought forth her first-born son, and wrapped him in swaddling clothes, and laid him in a manger; because there was no room for them in the inn.

And there were in the same country shepherds abiding in the field, keeping watch over their flocks by night.

And lo, the angel of the Lord ame upon them, and the glory of the Lord shone round about them; and they were sore afraid.

And the angel said unto them, Fear not: for, behold, I bring you good tidings of great joy, which shall be to all people.

For unto you is born this day in the city of David a Saviour, which is Christ the Lord.

And this shall be a sign unto you: Ye shall find the babe wrapped in swaddling clothes, lying in a manger.

And suddenly there was with the angel a multitude of the heavenly host praising God, and saying,

Glory to God in the highest, and on earth peace, and good will toward men.

And it came to pass, as the angels were gone away from them into heaven, the shepherds said one to another, Let us now go even into Bethlehem, and see this thing which is come to pass, which the Lord hath made known unto us.

And they came with haste, and found Mary, and Joseph, and the babe lying in a manger.

And when they had seen it, they made known abroad the saying which was told them concerning this child. And all they that heard it wondered at those things which were told them by the shepherds.

But Mary kept all these things, and pondered them in her heart.

Luke 2:1-20

MAN — WOMAN

"Man's love is of man's life a thing apart;
   'Tis woman's whole existence. Man may range
The court, camp, church, the vessel, and the mart,
   Sword, gown, gain, glory, offer in exchange
Pride, fame, ambition, to fill up his heart,
   And few there are whom these cannot estrange:
Men have all these resources, we but one, —
To love again, and be again undone."

Byron, from "Don Juan"

I'LL TAKE YOU TO YOUR HOME, KATHLEEN

I'll take you to your home Kathleen,
Across the ocean wild and wide.
To where your heart has ever been,
Since first I won you for my bride.
The smiles that once you gave to me,
I scarcely ever see them now:
But many and many a time I see
A darkning shadow o'er your brow.

ONE FLESH

Therefore shall a man leave his father and his mother, and shall cleave unto his wife: and they shall be one flesh.

King James Bible (Genesis 2:24)

O I'll take you to your home Kathleen,
To where your heart will feel no pain;
And when the fields are fresh and green,
I will take you to your home again.

To that dear home beyond the sea,
My Kathleen shall again return.
There where the old folks welcome thee,
Thy loving heart shall cease to yearn.
For sweeter sings the silv'ry stream,
Beside your mother's humble cot;
Where brighter rays of sunlight gleam,
There all your grief will be forgot.

O I'll take you to your home Kathleen,
To where your heart will feel no pain;
And when the fields are fresh and green,
I will take you to your home again.

I know you love me Kathleen dear,
Your heart is ever fond and true.
I always feel when you are near,
That life holds nothing dear but you.
The roses all have left your cheek,
I've watched them fade away and die:
Your voice is sad when e're you speak,
And tears bedim your loving eye.

O I'll take you to your home Kathleen,
To where your heart will feel no pain;
And when the fields are fresh and green,
I will take you to your home again.

Alfred M. Durham

A baby is God's opinion that life should go on.

Carl Sandburg (1878-1967)

WEDDING CEREMONY
(Conventional vows)

"You will please take each other by the right hand.

"John Jones, you take Jane Smith by the right hand in token of the covenant you now enter into to become her companion and husband, to love, honor, and cherish her, in sickness and in health, as long as you both shall live. And you hereby promise to observe all the laws, covenants, and obligations pertaining to the holy state of matrimony; and this you do of your own free will and choice in the presence of these witnesses, and as if you were in the presence of God?"

Answer in the affirmative.

"Jane Smith, you take John Jones by the right hand in token of the covenant you now enter into to become his companion and wife, to love, honor, and cherish him, in sickness and in health, as long as you both shall live, and promise to observe all the laws, covenants, and obligations pertaining to the holy state of matrimony, and this you do of your own free will and choice in the presence of these witnesses, and as if you were in the presence of God?"

Answer in the affirmative.

"By virtue of the legal authority vested in me (religious or secular designation), I pronounce you, John Jones and Jane Smith, husband and wife, legally and lawfully wedded for the period of your mortal lives."

Ring ceremony (single or double exchange, as is the case).

"May God bless your union with joy in your posterity and a long life of happiness together, and may He enable you to keep sacred the covenants you have now made.
"You may now kiss each other as husband and wife."

The formal text of the ceremony may vary considerably from couple to couple without distracting from its objective.

Author Index

Title Index

No Coward Soul is Mine, 117
No Escape, 88
Nobility, 60
North Star, 213
Not In a Silver Casket, 22
Not Knowing, 101
Novels, 57

— O —

O My Father, 181
Oberammergau, 160
Oh I Had Such a Pretty Dream Mama, 204
Old Business, 105
Older, 50
Old Saul, 35
Old Stoic, The, 117
On His Deceased Wife, 235
One Flesh, 264
One Life, 135
One Mother, 21
Only News I Know, The, 161
Opportunity, 125
Order of the Home, 252
Our Mountain Home So Dear, 144

— P —

Paddle Your Own Canoe, 122
Pageantry, 102
Parting, 57
Peace, 78, 135, 255
Pedigree, 102, 257
Phantom of Delight, 227
Philosophers, 92
Pilgrim Marriage, 249
Pity and Forgive, 248
Plant a Tree, 58
Poetry, 106
Portrait, 89
Power, 102
Praise, 170
Prayer to Persephone, 158
Prayers, 153
Privilege, 67
Puritan Lady, 25

— Q —

Queen, 248

— R —

Railway, 34
Rains of Spring, The, 54
Recuerdo, 126

Remembrance, 114
Reminders, 140
Renewal, 91
Restlessness, 252
Richer Than Gold, 246
Rock Me to Sleep, 79, 131
Rocked in the Cradle of the Deep, 152
Roman's Girl's Song, 16
Roses, 107

— S —

Scars, 132
Scatter Sunshine, 182
Sea and Air, 5
Secrets, 62
Self Analysis, 155
Self Destruct, 40
Sermons, 157
Shadows, 102
She Dwelt Among the Untrodden Ways, 234
Shepherdess, 104
She Walks in Beauty, 228
Silver Threads Among the Gold, 241
Sincere, 79
Sleep, 66, 128
Solitude, 45, 130
Somebody's Mother, 113
Someone's Man, 56
Song, 84, 133
Song For Our Flag, 14
Song of Elga, 98
Song of Thanks, 42
Song of the Settlers, 15
Sonnet XXIV, 94
Sonnet 232
Sonnet to Edgar Allen Poe, 95
Sorrow, 105
Souls, 53
Spanish Johnny, 9
Sphere of Women, 193
Spider and the Fly, The, 68
Spires of Oxford, The, 4
Springtime, 27
Star, The, 77
Start Now, 134
Still Falls the Rain, 154
Still Pulling, 127
Story of God, 157
Summon Bonum, 215
Sundown, 82
Superiority, 251
Susanna and the Elders, 87
Sweet is the Peace the Gospel Brings, 151
Sweet Sounds, 259

Illustration Index